I0788437

ISBN   978-1-9680270-4-9 (6x9 hardback)

The Survivor's Regression

Part I
The Maturity Gene

M.P. Hendy

Table of Contents

Chapter 1

A Loss of Humanity

David dropped his bags at the door before falling onto his bed. He had just renewed his security contract for another year, something he never wanted to do in the first place. Reaching in his pocket, he pulled out his phone and a letter he received from Sam months ago. Putting the letter aside, he unlocked his phone, and after hitting the message app, he began typing. "I just got home, and I'm going to take a nap," he texted. "Okay, then get some rest and let me know when you feel like talking," she replied. "I will. I love you," he responded. "I love you too," she replied. David threw his phone to the side and wanted to scream. After nine years of waiting, he was fed up, but she was the one person he couldn't let go of.

David sat on his bed, the afternoon sun casting long shadows, a stark reminder of his dwindling hope. Then, the world went dark. Not just a flicker, not a temporary dip, but a complete and utter blackout. The city plunged into silence. The hum of electricity vanished, replaced by an unsettling quiet, and with it, communication ceased. Cell phones, lifelines in the modern world, were rendered useless.

His heart lurched, downstairs, his mother, frail and struggling, relied on oxygen. His brother was out, unsure of when he would return. Panic clawed at him, but years of ingrained discipline kicked in. He retrieved his emergency rations and weapons from his storage unit, preparations he'd made, driven by a compulsive desire to do just a little bit more.

The following weeks were a blur as the city slowly descended into chaos, fueled by fear and desperation. The silence was punctuated by the sounds of struggle, of loss, of a world unraveling. His thoughts constantly drifted to his children. The gnawing worry for their safety became unbearable. Finally, driven by an overwhelming need to find them, he set out, leaving his mother and brother behind.

The journey was arduous, each day he drove was a battle against dwindling resources and escalating dangers. Nearly a month bled into a landscape stripped of its familiar comforts. Hope dwindled with each passing mile, replaced by a growing dread. As he finally reached Texas, the weight of his journey settling upon him like a shroud. But the relief he craved never came. The scene that greeted him was worse than anything he imagined. His son, along with his family, were massacred, for the food in their cupboards, and God knows what else.

He knelt there, amidst the ruins of his son's apartment, the silence amplified by the echoes of laughter he would never hear again. His pack and weapons suddenly felt heavy, useless against the crushing weight of his loss. He was a survivor, yes, but at what cost? He was alive, but what about his children? Bottling up his wrath, he immediately went to his ex-wife's house to find his youngest son. He eventually found her at her parent's house in the countryside, alone. Turns out, she wouldn't allow their children to stay there with firearms, because she didn't trust them with weapons.

David felt his conscience evaporate as every thought in his mind crashed like a house of cards. "You never trusted me as a husband, you never trusted me as a father, and because you never trusted my children, they're all dead," he said coldly. Standing up to leave, he heard her voice as she cried out to him. "Where are you going," she asked. David didn't respond as he pulled a pistol from his bag, pointing it directly at her. David grit his teeth as he fought the urge to pull the trigger, before dropping it on the ground. After leaving the house, he searched the property for food, sunblock and fuel cans, finding just enough to get him out of the state.

Stopping at a gas station in the middle of the day, he was confronted by an aggressive store clerk wielding a bat, but managed to barter one of his many pistols with a box of ammunition for more fuel, water and food. David was determined to make it to Sam, even though she had refused to see him in the past, these were extenuating circumstances.

Just over a week later, he finally arrived, but the southwest was even worse off than he thought, houses burned in the distance as he crossed over the reservation, finally reaching his destination. Fear began to fill his heart as he thought about what he might say, after all, he had waited long enough, and if she truly loved him, she might forgive him for showing up suddenly.

As he pulled up to the house, he was pleased to see the door and windows intact, but as he opened the door, he was struck hard by the overwhelming stench of rotten eggs, ammonia and shit. Covering his mouth, he searched each room, afraid of what he might find. As he cleared each room, his anxiety began to build up like an overwhelming pressure building in his brain, ready to knock him out in an instant.

Just as he entered the bathroom, he gagged, the putrid stench of decay filled the room, pulling back the shower curtain, he completely zoned out. The tub was full of a smelly decomposing soup, full of maggots and covered in flies, black with hints of crimson as a partially exposed skeleton lay suspended in it. David examined the body, noticing the long wavy blonde hair and exposed safety razor, now rusted on the bathroom floor. David wasn't sure if he wanted to throw up, cry, or scream at the sight in front of him. Leaving the house quickly, he stood on the porch, taking out another cigarette. "Well, you finally got to see her, and at least she didn't lie about having blonde hair." David laughed as tears ran down his cheeks.

Sitting on the porch, he lit a cigarette and pulled the letter from his pocket. As he read it, he considered how much pain he might have been spared, if he never met her, or what she would have said if he ignored her wishes to stay away.

"My Dearest David. I know, after all this time, after every rejection, every wall I built between us, these words must seem hollow, a cruel joke played by a ghost. But please, please hear me out. I'm writing this sitting on the edge of my bed, staring at the streetlights filtering through the blinds. I can't bring myself to be there, in your room, with you. Even though every part of me aches for it. It's taken me years, years of therapy, countless sleepless nights, and a terror that claws at my insides to even begin to understand why I pushed you away so vehemently. You, who were always a sun in my life, were too bright to bare."

"I see faces sometimes. In my dreams, in fleeting moments of waking, I see a flash of rough hands, a glint of steel. I feel the terror again, the absolute violation, even though it's just a glimpse, it leaves me breathless. It was another life, they say. A trauma buried deep within my soul, bleeding into this one. And you, David, with your open heart and unwavering gaze, felt like the biggest threat. You were the epitome of everything I feared, everything I desperately wanted but couldn't allow myself to have. Your love was too pure, too good. I didn't believe I deserved it, and worse, I didn't believe I was capable of protecting it, or myself."

"Please understand this, David: I love you. I have loved you every day I've known you. That's the truth. The reason I hurt you, was because I was damaged. The thought of facing you now, of seeing the man you have become after all you've been through, terrifies me. I'm desperately scared that I'll hurt you again. That I will let the past ruin the future. I am not ready to face you, and I do not know when I'll be better."

"If, after everything, after all the pain I've caused, you can find it in your heart to forgive me, please know that I want to try. I want to build a future with you, a future where the shadows don't have to win. But I cannot do that without your patience, your understanding, and your willingness to meet me where I am, even if that's still a world away from you. I am sure that I'll never be a whole person. However, I can assure that I want to be with you. Please tell me. Tell me if there is still a possibility. With a love that has always been yours, Sam."

After reading the letter, David used his lighter to set it on fire, dropping it inside the door of the house as he walked to his car. After nearly a month, he finally made it back across the country to his brother's house, unfortunately, he was too late. Without more oxygen, and clean air, she eventually succumbed to fatigue and died in her sleep, at least, that's what he hoped. Meanwhile, his brother had already decided to abandon his home, So David took the rest of his weapons and ammo from his room and went to the only place he could think of, to find his former coworkers on the military base nearby. In the seven years that passed, things had only gotten worse, and the world's population was reduced to a fraction of what it was.

David was searching the hollowed out remains of an abandoned outlet mall, looking for supplies and survivors. As the final light of the sun faded over the horizon, the wind began to pick up, and anyone brave enough to go out nowadays had to be ruthless, sparing no one a second thought.

Nobody knew for certain what caused this, but most theorized that a coronal mass ejection had some part in it. When the electrical and communication infrastructure went down, government officials put pressure on private businesses to fix the problem, but most only installed patches or repaired damages. Winter had just ended, and the weather was still cool, so nobody felt an immediate sense of foreboding and most trusted the government's promises to fix the problem. Survivalists and doomsday preppers thrived, but only for a short while. Most planned only for a few months, and even those that planned for longer, couldn't hold out for several years, because in the end, it took more than food and bullets to survive.

After walking nearly six hours, David began looking for a place to sleep during the day. As dawn approached, he sought a suitable place to rest along the way, finally settling on a school bus, abandoned in a tunnel. He knew someone had stayed there before, because aluminum foil had already been stuck to the windows. After searching every seat for squatters, he settled on a middle seat to the left, facing the East.

He had a routine, so preparing for bed only took about an hour. After preparing some food and washing up, he reached in his bag for more clothes. After dressing in clean undergarments, he loosely put on his outerwear and stowed his weapons and bag under the seat before laying down.

The jarring lurch of the bus yanked David from the precipice of sleep. It wasn't the familiar sway of wind buffeting the old vehicle, but the definite, groaning complaint of the suspension succumbing to new weight. Someone had boarded. Instinct, honed sharp by the brutal realities of this broken world, flared. Beneath the tattered cloth of his shirt, his fingers tightened around the grip of his pistol. He waited, breath held, a silent predator nestled amongst the decaying seats.

As expected, hurried footsteps crunched on the grimy floor. They passed his row, moving with a purposeful, almost frantic energy towards the back. He strained to hear, his ears picking up the faint rustle of fabric, a suppressed sigh. The newcomer was female. He pieced together the puzzle: She was either desperate to hide, or a refugee from the unrelenting sun, seeking a moment's respite in the dilapidated shell of the bus. It was barely mid-morning, yet the oppressive heat already clawed past the hundred-degree mark.

He rose, the movement fluid and silent. In his hand, the familiar weight of his wakizashi felt comforting. He advanced towards the rear of the bus, his senses on high alert. As he neared, the woman looked up, her eyes widening in a mixture of fear and resignation. She began to tremble. He stopped a few feet away, allowing her to gauge his intent. Her head hung low, as if she were already surrendering to whatever fate awaited her.

He saw the ghost of a beauty that had once been. The world, or perhaps the men in it, had been merciless. Scars laced her arms and neck, intricate tattoos snaked across her exposed skin. Despite the ravages of hardship, a curvaceous figure hinted at a time when she commanded attention, not fear. Her hair, long and dark, hung in tangled clumps around her face.

Without a word, she began to unbutton her blouse, her movements mechanical, her expression etched with a numb acceptance. A deep, weary sigh escaped her lips as she pushed the fabric from her shoulders. "Stop," David said, his voice sharp and unexpected. His word sliced through the heavy silence. She paused, her gaze remaining fixed on the grimy floor. "Aren't you going to fuck me?" The question was delivered with a chilling lack of emotion, a statement more than an inquiry. "Why would you think that?" he asked, genuinely bewildered.

She finally lifted her eyes, meeting his briefly before darting away. "Well, I don't have any food, and I don't have anything else of value." He sat down on the seat next to her, careful not to intrude. "What's your name?" A flicker of something – confusion? Relief? – crossed her face. "I don't remember," she whispered. "You don't remember?

Where are you from?" "I'm from Korea, but I was born in Thailand." "How did you wind up in Korea?" "My father is Korean, plus there was more work there," she explained, her voice gaining a fragile strength.

The conversation unfolded slowly, haltingly, over the next hour. She seemed utterly oblivious to the fact that she was still partially undressed, her shirt pooled around her waist. Perhaps the heat had numbed her to such concerns, or perhaps she was simply beyond caring. David tried not to stare, but the scars and tattoos were a roadmap of her suffering, impossible to ignore.

He learned she was an immigrant, lured to America with the promise of prosperity, ten years ago. She came to earn money for her family back home, but the harsh realities of survival had forced her down a darker path. She found work in the sex industry, a profession that paid well in a functioning society. But when the world fractured, the money she earned became worthless, and her only protectors were the men who had once been her clients.

As society crumbled, she became a sought-after commodity, her worth measured not in currency, but in access to dwindling resources. She drifted from place to place, desperate for food and shelter. Whoever offered her temporary refuge took what they wanted, using her until they grew tired of her, or until someone else came along with a better offer. It didn't matter who they were, or where she was. She had long since surrendered the illusion of control, allowing herself to be used as they saw fit. It was easier that way, a grimly logical path in a world devoid of hope.

David listened, his heart aching with the weight of her experiences. He wanted to help, to pull her back from the brink, but he recognized the hollow look in her eyes, the weary resignation that spoke of a spirit already broken. He suspected she didn't have much time left, that the relentless abuse had taken an irreversible toll.

He reached into his meager pack, pulling out a package of peanut butter, one of his most prized possessions. "Eat this for now and get some rest. I'll wake you up when the sun goes down. For now, I'll make sure that you're not disturbed." He said, his voice steady, attempting to convey a stoic strength he didn't entirely feel.

Tears welled in the corners of her eyes. She nodded, unable to speak. "Can I sleep with you?" she asked, the words barely a whisper, laced with desperate hesitation. "Why?" "Because you're so nice to me, and I think you're a good person." He shook his head gently. "No, you can't. If someone else comes, I want to be able to get to them before they get to you. So, for tonight, stay out of sight and sleep. I'll keep watch."

She stood up, a wave of vulnerability washing over her features. She moved to approach him, driven by a primal urge to express her gratitude in the only way she knew how. But David reacted instinctively, his movements precise and practiced. Like a rehearsed dance, he turned his body, gently guiding her towards an empty seat on the east side of the bus, furthest from the setting sun. He sat her down with a quiet firmness. "What's your name?" she asked, finally a glimmer of hopeful intrigue in her voice. "David," he replied. "David," she repeated, the name sounding unfamiliar yet strangely comforting on her lips. "David, I wish I would have met you sooner."

As the day wore on, the bus transformed into a stifling oven. The two of them, connected by shared humanity yet separated by the chasms of their experiences, retreated into a fitful slumber. David remained vigilant, his hand never straying far from his weapons, a silent guardian against the horrors that lurked outside the rusted shell of the abandoned bus.

David woke intermittently throughout the day, the uncomfortable bus seat and gnawing anxieties conspiring to steal any real rest. As he finally roused himself, he found her subtly closer. She had, while he dozed, shifted to the bench seat beside him, the backrest now the only barrier between them. The silent plea for proximity was obvious. He knew the grim task that awaited him, and the anticipation settled like a stone in his gut.

Earlier, when he'd first sat near her, her scent had struck him. His sense of smell was a curse and a gift, hyper-sensitive, able to discern nuances others missed. Now, that keenness delivered a chilling diagnosis: the faint, acrid tang of decay, a subtle undertone of sickness clinging to her like a shroud. Without advanced medicine and resources no one possessed anymore, her time was limited.

This was likely why she remained unattached, a burden no one wanted to bear in a world already teetering on the brink.

He stood over her, watching her sleep. Her face, usually etched with worry, was momentarily smooth, peaceful. This was likely the most restful sleep she'd had in a long time, and the thought pricked at his conscience. He nudged her ankle with his boot. "It's time to wake up."

Her eyes flickered open, darting around the unfamiliar space before settling on him. Recognition dawned, and a fragile, almost hopeful expression touched her lips. "Are you leaving?" she asked, her voice soft with a mixture of fear and anticipation. "We both are," he responded, his voice deliberately devoid of warmth.

She bit her lip, a valiant attempt to suppress a smile that didn't quite reach her eyes. Tears welled, blurring her vision. Dusk was approaching, and with it the dangers of scavenging parties and desperate souls. They had to leave, and quickly.

They disembarked from the bus, stepping onto the overgrown verge. As they rounded the back, David stopped, his hand a firm grip on her arm. "Listen," he said, his gaze unwavering. "There's something you need to understand before we go, alright?" "Okay," she replied, her voice barely audible. "I'll listen." "I don't have the resources," he stated, the words feeling like shards of glass in his throat, "or the space to take care of you."

A shadow of understanding passed over her face, a hint of resignation replacing the earlier hope. "I understand," she said, the sadness palpable in her tone. "But I'll at least take you away from all of this," he offered, the promise hollow, inadequate. "Uh huh," she murmured, her eyes searching his. "I trust you." She nodded, a small, fragile gesture of faith. "Close your eyes," he commanded, the words clipped and devoid of emotion.

She obeyed instantly, tilting her head back slightly, her face upturned as if welcoming a dream. David's gaze lingered on her. The curve of her neck, the way the fading light caught in the strands of her long, unkempt hair. The permanent etching of sadness that time and hardship had carved into her features. Yet, despite it all, she had almost smiled. He drew his wakizashi from its saya, the polished steel glinting in the dying light. The movement was swift, practiced, economical. In a single, clean stroke, he beheaded her.

Her body crumpled to the ground, the suddenness of it jarring. David stood for a moment, looking down at her lifeless form, a silent mourning etched on his face. "Such a waste," he thought, the sentiment echoing the despair that gnawed at him constantly. He knelt, wiping the blood meticulously from the blade with a portion of her tattered shirt. Sheathing the wakizashi, he turned and walked away without a word, without a backward glance.

The entire day was spent walking, the miles blurring into a monotonous rhythm of footfalls and labored breaths. It was early dawn when he finally reached his destination - a humble, utilitarian haven carved out of the ruins. His home, a renovated portion of an older clinic, was a testament to practicality over comfort.

The morgue in the basement had been transformed into a sterile storage facility, every surface scrubbed and disinfected. The ground floor offices were fortified, repurposed into barracks for the small group who called it home. The second floor, largely unused, occasionally served as a rudimentary hydroponics greenhouse, a desperate attempt to supplement their dwindling food supplies.

He entered the main room, fatigue pulling at his limbs. He emptied his pack onto the rough-hewn table, leaving the scavenged supplies for his roommates to sort. Elijah, his old coworker from before the world ended, emerged from the adjoining room. "What did you manage to find?" he asked, his voice weary. David answered quietly, avoiding eye contact. "Some ammo, dry food, and old cigarettes." Elijah grunted, his gaze distant. He turned and retreated to the kitchen, his movements slow and deliberate.

David lit a cigarette, the nicotine a temporary balm to his frayed nerves. He sat back on his cot, the rough fabric scratching against his skin. His mind drifted, a painful tide of memories washing over him. The life he had lost, the time he spent with his children, the faces of those he had cared about.

Was it all a waste? The only woman he truly loved, the woman he would have given anything for, could never give herself completely. He was consumed by anger, directed both inward and outward. Why didn't anyone trust him? He felt that the people in his life that he wanted to protect the most didn't trust him enough to let him, so they pushed him away, rejected him over and over again.

He carried this righteous indignation in his heart like a piece of armor, shielding his own vulnerability and feelings of inadequacy. Outwardly, he presented a mask of methodical efficiency, ruthless pragmatism, devoid of emotion. But these trips away from home, these brutal acts of mercy, were the only things that allowed him to vent his pain and frustration, keeping him just above the threshold of calm and homicidal insanity.

He removed his boots and outer garments, piling them neatly at the foot of his cot. He prepared for sleep, taking deep breaths to slow his pounding heart. Yet, secretly, he harbored a silent wish, a desperate plea for oblivion. He hoped, with a quiet desperation, that something would find him in the night, that death would claim him swiftly and painlessly. After all, everyone he had ever loved, everyone who had ever hurt him, was gone. And he had no real future to look forward to. He was simply existing, a ghost in a world haunted by the ghosts of what once was.

Chapter 2

Ghosts of the Future

David woke up, sweating in his sleep. But rather than the smell of dust and burnt ash, he could detect the faint stale smell of a child's bed, stained and worn from years of use. A soft tiger printed Biederlack blanket was wrapped around his legs and torso. He shot up, taking in the environment when he realized that he recognized his old room. Looking around, he felt disgusted at the child he once was. There were no pillowcases, there was no fitted sheet, clothes and toys littered the floor, and unfinished crafts were strewn about.

He climbed out of bed, looking around the house for anything he could remember. Had everything been a dream? Was this real? He heard before that some people suffering from a traumatic brain injury can conjure an entire life in their memory, when mere minutes pass in the real world, but even now, everything just felt too real. He left his room, searching the house for clues. It was the beginning of August, nearly half a year after his thirteenth birthday, most likely a weekday, because his parents' car was gone, and his brother was asleep in the other bunk bed.

He walked into the kitchen and made coffee. As he sat at the dining room table pondering over his situation, his brother came out of the bedroom and turned on the

Super Nintendo. He would stay there for several hours, until lunch, but David couldn't think about anything but the house. The random papers on the table, the dust on the floor, even the dirty dishes, he wanted to throw everything in the trash. As an adult, he had become a compulsive neat freak, and everything around him felt dusty and disorganized.

Unwilling to fester any longer, he got up and systematically, he went from room to room, cleaning everything in every room, other than his parents'. When he finished, he made a list, several groceries were needed and some things in his life that seemed trivial in the past, took on a whole new importance, while other things felt like a waste. His brother would ask several times if something was wrong, or if someone was in trouble, because he had never seen his brother so driven to clean and organize everything.

When his parents got home later that afternoon, they didn't say much about the clean house but were taken aback by David's proposition. He immediately handed over a shopping list. When had he become so proactive? What did he see or who did he talk to that motivated him to propose such requests? Rather than explain his thoughts or ideas, he simply went to his room and began taking out several sheets of loose paper.

He wasn't sure if this was a dream, but his memories never faded as they had before when he had a dream so vividly. Not only could he remember every detail, but he instinctively reacted to every sight and sound with the efficiency and discernment of an experienced paramilitary veteran. So, he started writing down significant events from his dream that he could use to prove his dream was real. The more he thought about it, the more determined he became. If this was real, he could avoid the mistakes he made before, but what about his children? If he married the same person, and got her pregnant on the same day as before, could he bring them back? If he avoided past mistakes, could he better prepare himself for the disaster to come? What about the people in his life he let slip away? The people he held grudges for?

There was no guarantee anything would work to his favor, even his current life seemed to make cultivation an uphill battle. His parents would never take him seriously, and he didn't have the money or the resources to do this on his own. Slamming his fist down, he cursed, spitting as he threw his pen and paper to the floor. Just then, his father opened the door, throwing it open as he yelled, "What the hell did you say?" His father grabbed him by the arm, pulling him to the living room, but before he got to the door, he grabbed his own wrist, and turned his body, pushing his own elbow into his father's armpit, breaking his hold.

His mother walked out, hearing the commotion. "Guess what your son just did." he asked, rhetorically. David snarled before anyone could respond. "What gives you the right to act so righteous?" He criticized both of his parents, pointing out their shortcomings, his father's drinking and drug use, his mother's misguided parenting tactics. "Am I not allowed to be frustrated at how things are? You always criticize my habits and hobbies!" pointing at his mother. "And you can't even pretend to be a good parent, unless we are of some use to you!" pointing at his father. Furious and frustrated, his father reached out to slap him in the face, but before his hand could make contact, David blocked his forearm with his left arm, then locked his own arm with his right arm, instantly stopping the assault.

The room was suddenly silent as his father tried to break free. After a moment he let go, apologizing for his outburst, and walked back to his desk. Shocked at David's response, his father didn't know how to react, he was used to his children fearing him. So, to have one of his own children stand up to him and subdue him so easily was not only unexpected, but terrifying as well. A few minutes later, after his father left his room, his mother sat on the edge of his bed.

"What is with you today? I spoke to your brother, and he said you spent the whole day cleaning." His mother asked, concerned. "I'm okay, I just had a really bad dream last night and now I feel like everything has changed." "Are you going to be okay?" she asked with a concerned expression. "I'll be alright, but I don't think I can be the same person I once was." His mother let out a deep sigh, "Was your dream that bad?" "It's not that it was bad, it just feels like I've lived an entire life already, and I can't help but mourn people that don't exist, and regret experiences that have never happened." His mother couldn't speak, unsure of how to reassure him. Instead, she stood up and patted his shoulder before leaving.

As he sat there contemplating his situation, he realized that not only had he retained the trauma and baggage he brought back with him, but also his knowledge, experience, endurance and even his strength and agility. It's as if his formerly matured maximal muscle force and cerebral development were grafted into this child-like body, extending the limits of his strength, endurance and brain. After all, he was a child again, ready to begin his life's cultivation, only this time, he had a significant head start.

David spent the next few weeks testing the limits of this advantage, and it seemed that while his body was small, he possessed incredible strength for his age, and his brain absorbed and retained information like a sponge.

One morning he woke up, a bag sitting on his desk. He reached into the bag and pulled out three composition notebooks, a package of pens and a calculator. He had asked his parents for these items, in addition to his school supplies for the next year. He recalled his bad luck in the past, nobody in his family kept a journal because no one in his family valued privacy, luckily, he immediately thought of a solution. As an adult, he learned Arabic and Spanish, and as a child, he learned to write Chinese Kanji and Greek letters, so he decided to employ the same tactics for encrypted note keeping he used when he was an interrogator. Back then, he created a simplified alphabet system, something that both humored and impressed his instructors.

He took out the first notebook and wrote a date across the top of the margin, the date the world ends. Here, he will write his account of how society fell apart, starting with that day, as well as his plans for surviving this calamity. He set the book aside and grabbed the second notebook. On the first line he wrote, "What I remember" This book will be a chronological account of his past life, categorized by event and key players. After setting this book aside, he grabbed the third notebook and wrote on the first page, "Journal." In this book, he will write a detailed account of his current life, leaving notes in the side margins for cross referencing.

His eighth-grade year was not as rebellious as he remembered it being. Rather than sneaking out with his friends and smoking, he would show up to class, finish his work quickly, and write in his notebook. Because his schedule was already set from the year prior, there was very little he could do about that.

One thing that did change was his social circle eventually broke apart. He couldn't pretend to be interested in the same things as was the year before, because for him, that was decades ago. When he woke up in the morning, he would warm up with a few calisthenics and stretches, make a small breakfast and leave for school. Occasionally his old friends would catch up to him. He played the role, despite having no actual interest in such things.

Despite the changes in his outlook and behavior, his old bullies remained. One way or another, he was going to face them. His first conflict was with Derek, someone who had started a fight with him in the gym. David retaliated when Derek slapped his face with his jacket from behind, and this brought a sense of resentment. Even though he kept his distance since then, Derek had always tried to provoke him at every opportunity. David made up his mind to make an example out of him at the next opportunity. One day, during gym class, they were on the basketball court, taking turns running shuttle sprints.

David was approached by a classmate, commenting on his thin physique, obviously attempting to start an altercation, but David didn't bite. When asked if he would ever fight, Derek chimed in, almost right on cue. "I'd fight you." David sighed, "And why is that? I thought we got along pretty well, before you decided to be an asshole for the sake of being an asshole." Derek was angry, insulted by his comment, but David refuse to participate. Out of nowhere, David's vision flashed black in a second, a volley of punches coming down on him. Grabbing Derek's wrist, he wrapped his arm around, striking him behind the shoulder before stomping down on his shin. David quickly had the upper hand, swiping his elbow at his neck before dropping his knees down onto Derek. Looking to his right, he grabbed Derek's wrist and lifted it, snapping his elbow under his weight.

The entire class was in an uproar, and David's counterattack took only a few seconds. The gym coach rushed over and pushed everyone out of the way. Everyone in the area, including the student that initially started the instigation, stood dumbfounded. David was in the right to defend himself, but did he have to ruthlessly break his arm? Clearly this was done in retaliation, not defense.

Needless to say, David was suspended from school for two weeks, and no one was going to press charges, because everyone clearly saw Derek attack first, not to mention the absurd number of hits David took before suddenly turning the tables. When he was sitting in the principal's office, he waited quietly for his father to pick him up, no longer fearing the repercussions of what anyone would say.

David thought back on his conversation with the assistant principal earlier. "Witnesses said that you broke his arm after you knocked him down, why didn't you stop and get a teachers attention?" "Because I've watched him do this repeatedly over the past few years, every time the adults simply side-stepped the issue, despite the amount of harm he caused for others. If I didn't take away his ability to fight, he would only continue with impunity." "His mother wants to press charges, but witnesses put all of the fault on him. If I were you, I would have stopped once he was down." "I would have, if I wasn't completely certain that he would retaliate later. This way, he won't be trying to punch anyone for the rest of the year." The assistant principal was exasperated, but didn't say more. He was well aware of Derek's past behavior, even though he only started working at this school that year.

David had been suspended several times the year prior, but this was for using profanity in front of the band director and assistant band director. Luckily, the current assistant principal had no knowledge of this. David considered this and was concerned that his reputation would already be tarnished. After all, for everyone this happened just last year, even though it was nearly 41 years ago for him. His father arrived, waving his hand quickly to get him up. The ride home was quiet, and nobody said a word.

His father had to go back to work, so he didn't stay, but left with an open promise. He and his mother would discuss their plan for him once they both had a chance to discuss it. Last year when he was sent home, his father brought him to work, leaving him in the car with assignments to keep him busy. Obviously, they didn't want him to have an at-home vacation during this time, but this situation was different, at least he had hoped. Later that evening he awaited a final decision from his parents. After dinner, he was beckoned by his parents and stood, waiting for their verdict.

His father spoke first, "You haven't been back in school for more than two months, and you've already been suspended. Your mother and I talked it over and we both understand why you did what you did but rewarding you with time off isn't a suspension." "May I speak?" Holding up his hand. "Go ahead, speak." "I understand why I was suspended, but I have been the target of bullying on a consistent basis. You tell me to stand up for myself, but when I do, I'm only targeted further. I did what I had to do because the teachers aren't going to protect the students, and their parents aren't going to discipline their children. So, I put a stop to the problem and potentially prevented who knows how many other students from being attacked. I don't regret my actions and if you decide that locking me up for the entire time is going to force me to reflect on my actions, it will not." "Then what would you suggest, should we just let you stay at home and do whatever you want?" his mother asked. "No, I'm not suggesting that, but I have an idea that might satisfy you while providing an experience similar to our criminal justice system."

David's parents both raised their eyebrows. They had never heard such an articulated response from their son before, so obviously, they were curious. "What do you think?" his father exclaimed. "If it's a good suggestion, we'll consider it." His mother added. "Community Service. There are nine school days left of my suspension, which is at least 54 hours of community service, if you consider lunch. There are nineteen houses on our block, so I have plenty of opportunities to serve." "What would you do, just clean their house?" his father retorted. "I don't think everyone would agree to that, but how about this, you write a statement, saying that I have been suspended from school, and my punishment is community service. I'll go door to door and get a schedule and you can verify my time each day." "What kind of work would you do?" His mother asked. "I don't think I'm in a position to complain, but if I suspect the work may be dangerous, I'll simply go to another house and get the time another way." "That actually sounds like a good idea." His father remarked. "I think it should be 60 hours, you know, just to round it off." His mother added.

In the two short weeks that followed, not only had he finished his community service, but he had also gone above and beyond, earning the trust and favor of more than half of his neighbors. Additionally, the long hours of hard manual labor had tempered his physical prowess. After his return to school, David would return to his neighbors' homes each weekend, this time working for pay. A benefit he sought to capitalize on, at least while he still had so few options available.

This continued for several months, earning enough money to buy his own clothes and even purchasing supplies that he would use for training and practice. In his past life, he only started to develop skills such as knife throwing, Muay Thai, sword fighting and bow hunting as an adult. This time, he would add to that knowledge and cultivate his skills as he matured. His time at school had changed as well, it seemed his actions had earned him a reputation for being ruthless, yet his teachers had no complaints. He would finish every assignment immediately, and even agreed to help others, as an attempt to curry favor with the faculty and staff.

As Spring came, David had established his reputation as a trustworthy pupil in school, as a dependable presence in the neighborhood, and as a ruthless and strong adolescent by everyone else. He led his own life with very little interference from his parents, as he had given them no reason to doubt. His grades were always high, yet he didn't seek any praise. He finished most of the housework on his own, and even prepared dinner several nights a week, so asking him to do anything seemed completely inappropriate. He worked for his own money and purchased his own clothes and supplies, so paying him an allowance seemed insulting. Summer quickly approached and as the school year ended, it was at this time, a new neighbor moved in across the street, Tiffany, a Highschool Junior, and her mother Connie.

His mother would often watch him as he went about his day, weeping quietly to herself, because she could hardly remember the last time she had seen him smile. In truth, David had already mourned for his family years ago. He not only knew how each of them would die but even cried himself to the point of exhaustion every time it happened, as far as he was concerned, they were only ghosts of his future. So, facing them now only reminded him of those moments, he couldn't do anything to help them then, and nothing he did now would save them in the future, so rather than dwelling on what he thought was already lost, he committed himself to saving those that he might have a chance to.

Chapter 3

The Inappropriate Crush

David had always remembered Tiffany as being genuinely kind. In a sea of girls who embodied the stereotypical blonde cheerleader – often vapid, concerned with popularity above all else – Tiffany stood apart. There was a quiet empathy about her, a lack of pretense that he found deeply attractive, even as a child. He harbored a secret fondness for her back then, a shy admiration that he never dared to voice. Years passed, and the imagined chasm between them – defined by age, social circles, and perceived differences – seemed insurmountable. He eventually resigned himself to being just an acquaintance, letting the embers of his childhood infatuation cool.

However, circumstance had a way of blurring the lines. They were both smokers, a shared vice born out of adolescent rebellion. Since neither was old enough to legally purchase cigarettes, they occasionally bummed them off each other. These brief exchanges became their justification for a sort of social camaraderie, a tenuous connection that barely scratched the surface. But this time felt different. For Tiffany, it was a new encounter, yet for David, familiarity had long been surpassed by a deeper understanding. This imbued him with a fearlessness, a maturity that belied his chronological age. She noticed it immediately – the way he carried himself, the steady gaze that didn't waver.

One sweltering summer afternoon, David knocked on Tiffany's screen door. He explained his self-appointed role as the neighborhood handyman, offering to tidy up her yard for a small fee. It was a transparent ploy, an orchestrated opportunity to spend time near her. Connie, who had been lounging inside, simply stated, "Sure, I guess." So David began working on pulling the weeds and mowing the lawn while Tiffany sat inside, watching him from the window.

After nearly two hours of sweaty labor, Tiffany emerged onto the back patio as the aroma of her mother's cooking wafted from the kitchen window. She pulled a cigarette from her pack, the familiar ritual a small act of defiance. "Want one?" she asked, her voice casual.

Eager to prolong the interaction, David accepted. He took a cigarette from her pack and settled into one of the faded plastic chairs. The two engaged in light conversation, a comfortable rhythm punctuated by the crackling of the cigarette and the distant sounds of Connie, Tiffany's mother, preparing dinner.

Connie glanced out through the kitchen window, a knowing smirk on her face. She remembered her own teenage years and the endless quest for connection. "You're going to our high school in the Fall?" David asked, breaking the comfortable silence. "Yes, I just moved here," she replied, exhaling a plume of smoke. "What grade will you be starting?" "Eleventh. It's gonna suck starting in the middle of high school." "You'll do fine," David said with uncharacteristic confidence. "I'm sure your friends will visit, and you'll make new friends here easily." "How are you so sure?" she challenged, a playful glint in her eyes. "Because you don't have to work your way up like everyone else. You're going to be the new girl, that makes you mysterious."

She smiled, genuinely impressed by his insight. "Thanks. What about you?" "Ninth grade, but I'll be okay." "Damn," Tiffany chuckled. "I thought you might be older. Do you have a lot of friends?" David paused, a shadow passing over his face. "Maybe I am older than I look. But no, I don't have very many friends." "What about the people you talk to? Aren't y'all friends?" "I suppose," he conceded, "but that feels like such a long time ago. I think I might have outgrown their antics." "It's good to have friends," Tiffany said, her tone softening. "What happened? Did y'all have a fight?" "No, nothing like that. Let's just say that I woke up one day and saw everything differently."

He struggled to articulate the shift in perspective, the growing awareness of his unique way of processing the world. "Well," Tiffany offered, standing up after extinguishing her cigarette, "I can be your friend if you want." "Tiffany, can I use your bathroom?" David asked, abruptly changing the subject, a habit he often employed when emotions became too intense. "Sure, it's the first door on the right."

David snuffed his cigarette and walked through the back door. After pulling off his work boots, he smiled politely at Connie, who was humming softly over the stove, and disappeared into the bathroom. After washing his hands, he lingered for a moment in the kitchen, observing Connie's culinary efforts. She was braising pork chops in a skillet, the rich aroma filling the air. David's brow furrowed. "Can I help you with that? I'm actually quite the cook," he offered, his voice laced with genuine enthusiasm. Connie raised an eyebrow, surprised by the offer. "Oh, you're quite the cook, huh? What would you suggest?"

David's gaze darted around the kitchen, assessing the available ingredients. He opened the refrigerator and extracted a stick of butter and a bottle of vinaigrette, placing them strategically next to the stove. He carefully cut a pat of butter for each pork chop and deftly turned down the flame on the burner. As the butter melted into a golden pool, he gently turned each pork chop, drizzling a small amount of vinaigrette over the top. Placing a lid over the skillet, he transferred it to the oven, preheating it to a low heat.

Connie watched, her initial skepticism slowly giving way to intrigued curiosity. "Well, I never would have thought of that," she admitted. David, ready to finish his work outside, put on his boots. Just before he walked out the door, he turned back to Connie and said, "Take the pork out in about fifteen minutes. It will be juicier."

Connie remained apprehensive at first, unsure of what to make of David. But after spending several hours observing him work, she was impressed. He was not only a hard worker, but he also possessed a remarkable ingenuity and a knack for problem-solving. He required little to no direction, a quality rarely seen in boys his age. Even her daughter seemed to enjoy his company. His work ethic and quick pace gave her a reason to invite him back the next weekend.

Very soon, Connie and Tiffany came to expect David's regular visits. With just the two of them living in the house, having a male presence, even a young one, seemed to bring a sense of balance. His attire was also not typical for a boy his age, but rather, it was fitted for his body and neutral in color, lacking any sense of flash or flair. He spoke beyond his years and displayed a confidence that made him instantly likeable. He started teaching Tiffany how to food prep, explaining the convenience and savings, as well as the health benefits compared to takeout. Tiffany was almost jealous at the way her mother talked about David. He didn't come to see her, but to earn a bit of extra money during the summer. However, for the few hours he was there each week, he basically got paid an allowance, even though she got the same, and had to do chores every day.

Every now and then, Tiffany would see him across the street, usually working diligently in someone else's yard. She even wondered if his parents were overly strict, driving him to work so relentlessly. One early afternoon, she beckoned him over, deciding to confront her curiosity rather than let it fester. "Hey Tiffany, did you need something?" "No," she said, "I just wanted to chill with you for a bit."

"Okay." He sat quietly for a few moments, observing her intently. A comfortable silence settled between them before they began engaging in small talk. During which time, he explained his compulsive desire to clean, even admitting he wasn't always like this. He never mentioned his Aspergers, as it had only recently been recognized in the DSM-5 and would not be considered as common for another 19 years. Even David himself wasn't fully aware of his condition until his 40's.

The two continued to talk about many things and over time, Tiffany had learned to appreciate David's insight and opinion. He was an open book of experience and captivated her every time he spoke. Tiffany found it very difficult to see him as her junior, even though he did look younger, nothing else about him compared to his peers, who she would often see walking around the neighborhood. Initially she thought his antics were amusing, but it didn't take long for her to realize that this wasn't some overplayed act, he really was as smart and capable as he led on, and something about him intrigued her.

She didn't see him much during school, because the freshmen were usually separated from the rest of the students. David, however, navigated the school with complete familiarity. Unlike the other freshmen, he was bold when he spoke to others, quick as he maneuvered the hallways, and efficient while he was in class. He didn't change his classes too much from last time, this was because he intended on keeping his life as similar as he remembered.

His experiences made him a natural leader, putting him on the front line of nearly every group assignment, lab and project. His days as a shy and introverted teen were long gone, this time, he was proactive, confident and popular. David didn't care who he was around, he would sit with anyone, talk to everyone and every time a fight broke out near him, he was surprisingly quick to neutralize it. This garnered him a reputation that would follow him, yet he preferred to be alone. His interactions with Tiffany made other classmates envious. Not that he sought her out, but because she did not hold back when she saw him at school.

Tiffany joined the drill team and met some friends there. As the topic of boys came up, Tiffany's mind immediately went to David, after all, her parents were divorced, and he was the most significant male presence in her life. She was apprehensive about talking about him at first, mainly because of his junior status, but as the conversations evolved, she found creative ways to fold him into the topic, intentionally keeping his identity a secret. Girls this age often went after older guys, but in Tiffany's mind, even they seemed immature.

One afternoon, as they cleaned up after practice, Tiffany's friend Sandra confronted her. "You mention this guy all the time, and so far, the only problem with him is that he doesn't own a car and still lives with his parents. Which is still better than most, so is he interested in you?"

Tiffany hung her head, feeling a blush creep up her neck. "I don't know. It doesn't seem like he's interested in anyone." "Are you interested in him?" Tiffany thought hard, chewing on her lip. "I don't know, but I've never met anyone like him. I can usually tell if a guy likes me, but he's unreadable, and he's a bit intimidating." "How is he unreadable?" Sandra pressed, her curiosity piqued. "He looks angry all the time, but when he talks, he's so friendly. And like, he smiles when he gets excited about stuff. Plus, he's really smart, and I can't think of anything he doesn't know."

Sandra grinned, recognizing the telltale signs. "It kinda sounds like you have a little crush on him. Maybe you should find out what he thinks about you?" Tiffany initially thought David would be an easy person to figure out, but the more she learned, the more she realized she didn't know. Eventually, her interest became an obsession. She learned about his notebooks, but she never knew what was in them. She even heard stories about him from other neighbors, including his peers – tales of his unusual intelligence and unwavering determination. This only fueled her curiosity.

Ultimately, the only person that could give her any helpful information about him would be him. But how does she confront him? What would she say if he asked her why she wanted to know so much? Thinking about this seemed absurd. Why was she so afraid of confronting a boy nearly two years younger than her? He was her friend, wasn't he? Then again, was his affection platonic?

One afternoon, David was sitting in the library during lunch and Tiffany sat in front of him, something he had never experienced nor expected. He put his pen down and closed his notebook. "Is there something you need from me?" At this point, he had made himself a significant presence in her life and somehow never showed any ulterior motive or purpose. "Can I give you a ride home today? There's some-thing I want to talk to you about." "Sure, we can do that," he replied without much thought.

It had been almost a year since they met, and he thought she would have gotten pulled into her social cliques at this point. After school, he waited in front of the school, notebook in hand, sitting on the concrete barriers alongside the stairs. He knew where she parked, but did not show his hand. She walked up to him, backpack over her shoulder, keys in hand, "Ready to go?" "Are you?" he reversed the question.

She let out a huff and before she turned, he grabbed the bag off her shoulder and started toward the parking lot. As they approached the parking lot, he cut in front of her, using his right arm to guide her to his right side. Before stepping onto the street, he grabbed her by the wrist and kept her positioned just behind his right shoulder as they walked to her car. She didn't say anything but looked almost lost at his actions. He hadn't hit his growth spurt yet, so she stood several inches taller than him, but still followed without making a fuss. On the ride home, the two sat in silence for a few minutes. "What did you want to talk about?" "What do you write in that book of yours?" she interjected. "Huh? Oh, I don't really want to talk about it, you'll just think I'm weird." He said, looking at the cover of the notebook. "I already do, but that's not a bad thing. If you don't want to tell me, you don't have to." He smiled, "Maybe I will someday." Tiffany curled her lips in a slight smile and kept driving. Both sat quietly again for a few minutes until they eventually got to her driveway. "Thank you for the ride, I'll see you later."

As he reached for the door handle, she reached out and grabbed his forearm quickly. "Wait, I still want to talk to you." "It wasn't about the book?" "No, I was only curious, but I didn't want to talk in the car while I was driving." "Oh, then shall we talk inside, because sitting in the car might look creepy." Tiffany chuckled as she shook her head. "You're creepy enough for the both of us." Without saying a word, David left the car and waited at the top of the stairs next to the front door. Tiffany unlocked the door and pushed it open as David held the screen door open behind her, then followed her in after she entered. He removed his shoes at the door and waited as she got a drink from the refrigerator.

"Would you like something to drink?" "Thank you, I'll have tap water if that's okay." She had long since given up on questioning his choices and simply filled a plastic cup with water. She handed him the cup of water and sat down on the couch, posturing herself as if she was about to begin an interview. David took a sip of his water. "What is it you wanted to talk about that you couldn't talk about in the car?" She paused before responding, "I guess I wanted to know why I feel intimidated by you." She said in a mumbled voice. "Why would you feel intimidated by me, you're a few years older than me, plus, how am I supposed to respond to that as a question?" "I don't know, I just thought if we could talk about it, I would figure it out. I know you're younger than me, and I can clearly see that, but it really doesn't feel like that's the case."

David looked to the side, taking another sip of water. This gave her a moment to breathe as his eye contact seemed to make her feel vulnerable. "I think I know what you mean, and I'm sorry if I made you feel uncomfortable. I have my reasons, and I'll tell you if you want to know." She inhaled sharply, unsure of what kind of response to expect. "I'm not uncomfortable, you're just a bit intimidating. Plus, you're really smart and even my mom likes you. You're always exercising, and I know you're strong, because I've seen you work, but you're so thin and you know how to cook and you know so much stuff, but you don't really smile, plus you're so respectful to everyone, but you don't help anyone else and…" David stopped her, "Hold on, slow down. Sometimes I forget that you're a teenage girl."

Tiffany looked at him exasperated. Seeing her frustration, he let out a deep sigh before explaining further. "Yes, I am younger, but you know what I meant. Look, I do like to help others, but I don't like doing anything in vain. I help out, because I get paid. Earning their trust has little to do with my feelings on the matter and more to do with my long-term goals. However, you and your mother are genuinely kind, and I wanted to know you better while I had the chance."

"Why don't you like the others? Don't you think that's a little immature? Besides, I thought they all liked you." "I am immature, I'm fifteen, and my purposes for helping them are strictly for financial benefit." "Bullshit, nothing you do is immature, you have a reason why, and I want to hear it." "Okay, if you really want to know…"

David spoke in exhausting detail, revealing details about the neighbors and even including his own parents. He knew from his own past experiences that his efforts would not only go unappreciated, but would ultimately cripple his own self-worth, something he still struggled with from his past life. Tiffany stared intently as he explained, her body almost unable to move at the detail and conviction in his voice.

"Are we going to discuss the neighbors, I thought this was about you?" She took a deep breath, "It is, I just hoped maybe you had a crush on me or something, but now I don't know." She said, blushing slightly. "It would be better if you were a few years older." "I suppose that makes sense, but I think we're too young." "Are you kidding me, how am I too young?" he held up his hand, "Obviously you're older than me, but I don't think even you are ready for this, so I'm certainly not old enough."

She looked inquisitively into his eyes as she clenched her thighs, her fingers wedged between her legs. His aloof posture showed no signs of discomfort, and her curiosity began to claw at the back of her mind. "Ready for what, going out, a relationship, sex?" Unprovoked by her words, David simply took another sip of his water, clearly not shaken by her question. "Yes, and seriously? You said that on purpose, didn't you?" "I just wanted to see your reaction." Side stepping the accusation. "Relationships aren't supposed to be a joke, if you're not ready to give in completely, why waste the opportunity?"

She remained silent, biting her lip. David finished his water and stood up. He handed her the empty cup and thanked her for the water before putting on his shoes and walking home. Not dissatisfied with his conversation, David still felt the heartbreak caused by his past relationships, he knew Tiffany would be leaving after Highschool, and at the present, he was simply too young. David didn't have any homework as usual, because he always finished it at school before coming home. He rummaged through the refrigerator before pulling out ingredients to make dinner. Something his parents had gotten used to.

Chapter 4

Behind Closed Doors

Weeks had passed and David was in front of his house, sweeping the sidewalk and porch when Tiffany stepped out of her front door, sitting down on the front porch before lighting up a cigarette. David paused as he noticed and realized she was looking right at him. She lifted her hand, gesturing for him to come and keep her company. He placed the broom in the corner of the porch and opened his front door. "Mother, I'm going across the street for a few minutes." He closed the door and crossed the street, staying off the grass and watching her as he approached her. This made her lower her head slightly, afraid of making eye contact.

"Why invite me over of you're afraid to look at me?" "Fuck you, I'm not afraid of you. You just look like a kid when you're sweeping, and I thought it was cute." "I am a kid." "You want one?" holding out her pack. "No thank you, my mothers in the living room and I don't want her to see me smoking." "Oh. Hey, I got a job!" "I know, at the waterpark." "How did you know?" "Because your friend works there, and it just seems like the most obvious answer." "Liar, someone told you." "You're right, I am lying, but no, no one told me. I'm proud of you though, I think you'd look good in a swimsuit." "You wanna see?"

Jumping to her feet. "Right now?" "Yes, right now." She pulled him to his feet and they both walked inside. He immediately took off his shoes as she skipped down the hall to her bedroom. Just as he sat down, he heard her calling from her room. "Come on!" "You aren't going to bring it out here?" "No, come here, I don't want to walk back and forth."

David stood up, taking a deep breath as if his body weight doubled. As he walked down the hall, he could see her getting changed through the open door. Why didn't she close the door? Does she not care if I see her change? Curious about her intent, he didn't hesitate to walk into her room. Standing by the door, he watched as she pulled the swimsuit up over her shoulders. It was a bright red one piece, suitable for a lifeguard at a public pool.

"Ta-daa, what do you think?" "I think that you knew I would see you getting dressed." he responded coldly. Tiffany acted embarrassed, but David was having none of that. "Stop acting like you didn't know what you were doing, you knew damn well I could see you and you set this up." She hung her head, embarrassed that she had been caught. "I'm sorry, I wasn't trying to tease you like that, I swear, I just..." he interrupted her, "Stop, don't finish that thought. It doesn't matter what you thought, you took a risk, acting that way in front of a boy. How do you know I'm not a terrible person?" She sat on the floor, "I don't know how I know; I just do. You're a conundrum, I guess it might have been different if I didn't get to know you so soon after meeting you, but I don't think you would hurt anyone." He put on a serious face, "You're wrong, I am more than capable of hurting others."

Tiffany looked at him with sarcastic doubt. "Sure, if you say so." "There, that's that false sense of security that will put you in danger. You think I don't have the mental of physical capability to hurt someone, or kill someone?" "I didn't mean that, I just meant that, well, … It's just, I don't feel danger when I'm around you." David thought for a moment, perhaps I can use this opportunity to scare her, maybe then she'll be more careful. "Do you want to put that to the test?" She looked at him, confused. "How would we do that?" "Simple, I'll show you how dangerous I can be. Even with two handicaps." "Two?" "Yes, first, you can do anything and everything to stop me, and I won't resist." "What's the second?" "I promise not to hurt you, not even a little." She was completely skeptical, but she was very curious to see what happens."

He went outside onto the porch and shut the door. After a few seconds, he knocked, Tiffany giggled before opening the door. As soon as the door opened, David rushed her, she didn't even get a second to respond. He effortlessly put her into a submissive position within seconds, and before she knew it, she was on the ground. In only a few moments, he gagged her, bound her arms behind her back, and even tied her feet behind her, using only a t-shirt and the laces from her shoes. Every time she pulled, everything got uncomfortably tight.

She thought she was going to get a show, but this was terrifying. "Now that you can't do anything to stop me, I can do anything I want to you." He said sinisterly before he reached down and untied her. She knew she wasn't in danger, but this experience was a wake-up call. He knelt and picked her up like she was a small child, carrying her to her room. In the short distance from her living room to her bedroom, she held onto him tightly. He set her on her bed, but she didn't let go. David realized that after experiencing such an act, she needed to calm her emotions. "It's okay, you can take your time." He cradled her in his arms, holding her close to himself for nearly five minutes.

She finally let go but refused to get off his lap. He wanted to say I told you so, but he thought better of it. "Are you alright?" he asked. "I'll be okay," She turned her body to face him, wrapping her arms and legs around him. "Uh, Tiffany?" "I just need a few more minutes, that was scary." A few more minutes passed, and David felt something wet on his shoulder. Was she crying? Did she fall asleep and start drooling? He was about to ask but felt her breath behind his ear. "Tiffany, I can't be caught in your room like this." She slowly let him go, and he left the room. A few seconds later, she heard the front door opening and closing.

She looked out onto the porch and after seeing him light a cigarette, went out to join him. "I thought you didn't want your mom to see you smoke." "She's not watching." David handed a cigarette over his shoulder, she took it and sat beside him, leaning her head against him. "Would you ever hurt me?" she asked. He took a drag off his cigarette before answering, "Would I ever have to?" She shook her head, "No sir." After finishing his cigarette, he flicked off the cherry and got up to leave. She waited on the porch, watching him go back to sweep the sidewalk.

Months passed and school was out for the summer. Tiffany, who only worked weekends during the school year, was working weekdays during the summer vacation. On weekends, her friends would come over and David stayed in the house when he wasn't working odd jobs. He didn't want to get pulled into their drama. Occasionally, he would catch her watching his house but hardly went to see her. She would turn eighteen in the fall, and he was still only fifteen. David was doing calisthenics in the living room when his mother announced that they would be going to the waterpark on Saturday. He sighed at the thought, after all, he remembered this day specifically and knew it was going to be a drag. Then he had an idea, he put on his shoes and ran across the street to Connie's house. After knocking on the door, she answered excitedly. "David, good to see you. Would you like to come in?" "Yes ma'am, but only for a moment." "Coffee or water?" "Coffee sounds good, Thank you."

She had become familiar with his habits and tastes, so when he visited, she always offered him a beverage. "I'm glad you came over, but I wish Tiffany were here, she's been missing you." "Don't tease me like that, you know I'm just a kid." "Well, that's what you say. So, what brings you over?" "Actually, it's about your daughter." "Oh?" "Not like that. Your daughter works at the waterpark and since Tiffany works there, I figured she would know about any specials or discounts available." "I'm not sure dear, but I'll ask her when she gets home. When are you going?" "Mother said Saturday." "I'll ask her and let you know before then." "Okay, thank you." "No problem."

After finishing his coffee, David left and went back home. He relayed his plan to his mother and got back to what he was doing. The afternoon passed and so did dinner. As he was clearing the table, someone knocked on the door. After answering the door, his father announced, "David, it's the neighbors for you. Let your brother finish clearing the table and see what she wants." David turned off the porch light after seeing who it was and stepped outside. "What are you doing here, I thought your mother was going to talk to me later. Didn't you just get home?" "Yes, but I thought this would be easier." "Okay, but I feel bad now for having you come over yourself." "No, this is something I should do myself." She reached into her bag and pulled out a handful of plastic bracelets, handing them to David, smiling like she found his lost keys.

"What are these?" he asked. "These are the access bracelets for Saturday." "How do you know they'll use this color?" "Because my friend is dating the manager, and she told me." "Clever girl," mumbling to himself. "Well, thank you so much, this will definitely be appreciated. Is that all?" "Mmhmm," she nodded. "Can I walk you home then?" "Yes sir," she said coquettishly.

He held her hand as he walked her across the street and led her to her door. When he reached her door, he felt her bump into his back, her body pressing against him suddenly. "Oh, I'm sorry for stopping so suddenly." David exclaimed. "It's cool, thank you for walking me home." He thanked her again before turning around and going back home. As he went back into the house, he handed the bracelets to his mother. "What are these?" she asked. "These are the access bracelets for Saturday, so we don't have to pay admission to get in." "Are you serious, you didn't have to pay her for them?" his father asked. "Yes, and no, she just gave them to me for free." His parents looked at each other before his father spoke, "It looks like there's more to it than that." "What are you talking about?" "Go look at the back of your neck," his mother added. He ran to the bathroom mirror, uncertain of what he might find, until he saw the punchline. Right on the back of his lower neck, was a pair of apple colored semi-gloss lip prints. She had marked him.

Saturday had come quickly, and David had planned the day, trying to avoid the same problems as before. His mother packed the barbeque equipment and everyone else just got ready. As he packed a change of clothes and sunblock, his father loaded everything into the Firebird. After nearly an hour of driving, they finally arrived. Mother had passed out the bracelets and everyone was ready to go.

David was the only one that packed a backpack and before anyone asked, he grabbed the cooler full of food and started toward the entrance. His mother and father looked at each other, then back at David before closing the car and walking to catch up. David made his way to the back of the picnic area and cleaned out the barbeque pit. By the time his father arrived with the charcoal briquettes, David was already applying sunscreen over his arms and legs. The rest of the setup went smoothly as David and his mother set up the cooking area, his father and his two brothers had already left for the waterpark, and he finally took a moment to sit down.

"You can go swimming now; you don't have to stay here and keep me company." "I know, I'll go in a few minutes, I just wanted to make sure everything was good to go before I left." "You've already helped so much; you should be having fun." "I am having fun." His mother didn't say another word, after all, what could she say? Seemingly overnight, David seemed to have lost his childish ambitions. Not that she could complain, his grades in school were remarkable, he did his chores and then some, he even cooked and helped with the grocery shopping. Thinking on this, his mother couldn't help but become emotional, fighting back tears, she missed her rebellious middle child.

David started toward the waterpark, a familiar ache settling in his chest. The weight of reality seemed lighter when he shed his hat and t-shirt, leaving them on a nearby bench like discarded armor. His first stop was predictable, a magnetic pull he couldn't resist: the waterslide. He grabbed a faded yellow tube, its surface worn smooth from countless riders, and began the ascent. Each step up the metal stairs was a step back in time.

On his way up, the cheerful screams and splashing faded into a dull hum as his thoughts spiraled downward. His own children swam into his mind, their faces blurring at the edges of his memory. Almost nine years. Nine years since he'd last held them, laughed with them, tucked them into bed. Nine years since the world he knew had shattered, scattering the pieces beyond his reach. A wave of guilt and longing washed over him, threatening to drag him under.

"Go!" The lifeguard's sharp command cut through his reverie like a knife. David had dazed off, lost in the labyrinth of his past. The single word was a brutal, unwelcome return to the present. He gripped the tube tighter and pushed off, plunging into the swirling vortex of the yellow slide. Water splashed around him, momentarily stealing his breath as he careened downwards. The whoosh of the slide and the spray in his face were a temporary reprieve, a fleeting escape from the relentless gnawing within.

As he crashed into the shallow water at the bottom, the turbulent surface gradually calmed. He floated aimlessly in the manmade river, observing the other patrons with a detached curiosity. This wasn't some carefully curated romcom fantasy, teeming with perfectly tanned bodies and effortless charm. This was the messy, unfiltered reality of summer at a local waterpark.

The only genuinely attractive people were either working as lifeguards, their eyes constantly scanning the water, or conspicuously absent, likely seeking refuge in air-conditioned havens. Reality was a kaleidoscope of mismatched colors, protruding rolls stubbornly defying swimwear, and skin burnt to a lobster-red hue. Pale, overweight men sported oversized t-shirts, their faces betraying a mix of self-consciousness and forced enjoyment.

"David!" The sound of his name startled him, jolting him back to the present. He looked around, scanning the crowd for the source. "David!" The voice was closer this time, laced with a familiar impatience. "Tiffany, what the hell? I thought you were off today." He pushed himself to a standing position, water streaming down his face. "I volunteered for overtime," she replicd, her voice carrying a hint of defiance.

Standing on the side of the pool, her lifeguard uniform clinging to her frame, she looked taller, more imposing than he remembered. "Uh huh?" "I start my break in twenty minutes." She crossed her arms, raising an eyebrow. "Okay, so what?" He feigned indifference, though a knot of anxiety began to tighten in his stomach. What was she planning?

She put her fists on her hips, not saying a word, her gaze unwavering. The unspoken message hung heavy in the air. "Alright, alright." He sighed, surrendering with a weary resignation.

David immediately got out of the pool, deliberately avoiding her eyes. He tossed the tube onto the growing pile, its plastic surface slick with chlorine. He walked back to the designated barbeque site, the concrete burning against his bare feet. He dried off quickly with his threadbare towel, the familiar scent of chlorine and sunscreen clinging to the fabric. He put on his hat, pulling it low over his brow, then slipped into his t-shirt and sandals, a uniform of anonymity. He walked back towards the waterpark, the sounds of laughter and splashing a constant, irritating buzz in his ears.

He leaned against the rough, brown-stained wooden shed nestled beneath the imposing structure of the waterslides. He reached into his backpack, carefully extracting a plastic cigarette case. He had kept them hidden there, a small, forbidden comfort for moments like these. He lit a cigarette, the familiar burn a small act of rebellion against the relentless cheerfulness that permeated the air.

As he inhaled, the shed door swung open with a creak, momentarily obscuring the sunlight. He glanced up, recognizing the man who emerged. "Hey Brian." He offered a casual greeting, his tone deliberately neutral. The man, hearing his name, responded impulsively, "How's it going?" Brian didn't recognize David, his face a mixture of confusion and vague politeness. He likely assumed David was a colleague, based on his nonchalant greeting and aloof posture. David knew this was Brian, the boyfriend-manager of Tiffany's friend, Sandra.

"Oh, you're here! Come inside." Tiffany's voice, sharp and expectant, cut through the air. She arrived beside Brian, a determined glint in her eye. She pushed past him, opening the door wider and beckoning David inside. They both entered, leaving Brian standing outside, a bewildered expression on his face.

David sat at the picnic table in the middle of the shed, his gaze fixed on the weathered surface of the bench beneath him. He traced the grain of the wood with his fingertip, his mind searching for something that wasn't there.

He was looking for writing on the bench, a specific inscription, a symbol of a future that both was and wasn't his. Something he wouldn't see for another year, at least. It wasn't there. Without looking up, his voice flat and devoid of emotion, he asked, "Did you plan this?" She paused before answering, her gaze searching his face. "No, but I thought it would be funny." A nervous smile played on her lips.

"I got your message." He acknowledged, still focusing on the wood grain. She looked pleased, a glimmer of triumph in her eyes. "Did you? What did you think?" "I think my parents thought it was funnier than I did." He finally met her gaze, a hint of amusement flickering in his eyes. "Oh, I'm sorry," she said sarcastically, the edge in her voice barely concealed. She clearly wasn't sorry at all.

She locked the door behind her back, the click of the bolt echoing in the small space, and sat behind him on the bench, leaning her head against his back. The unexpected contact sent a jolt through him. "I thought we'd been over this already?" He sighed, the scent of her sunscreen and pool water filling his nostrils. "I know, you're just a kid, you keep reminding me." Her voice was muffled against his back. "Then get off of me." He shifted uncomfortably. "I will, just give me a moment." She tightened her grip on his arm. "Fine," he acquiesced, his shoulders slumping in defeat. He knew arguing was pointless.

Every time David tried to pull away, Tiffany would hold him tighter, her grip surprisingly strong. For nearly ten minutes, neither of them moved, the silence punctuated only by the distant screams and splashing from the waterpark. The air in the shed felt thick and heavy, charged with unspoken desires and simmering frustrations. "Your break's going to be over soon." He finally broke the silence, his voice strained. "No, I get thirty minutes." She replied, her voice petulant. "Well, I don't." He shifted again, trying to dislodge her.

Tiffany huffed, a pouting expression momentarily flashing across her face. Then, suddenly, the door began to shake violently as someone tried to open it from the outside. "Just a minute!" She quickly got up and unlocked the door, her cheeks flushed. Standing outside was another lifeguard, slightly taller than her and holding a Sprite in his hand, his face a mask of polite curiosity. "Am I interrupting?" he asked, his tone carefully neutral. "No, we were just finished talking," she replied, her voice high-pitched and slightly flustered.

As they were talking, David headed toward the door, deliberately avoiding eye contact with the newcomer. "I'll head out." He walked out, leaving Tiffany and the other lifeguard standing there in the doorway, their conversation trailing off behind him.

During lunch, his mother prepared the food, and everyone sat down to eat. His little brother ate a hot dog out of order and everyone else ate hamburgers. Before getting up, his father asked, "Doesn't our neighbor Tiffany work here?" David responded coldly, "Yes, she's working today." His father nudged him teasingly, "Why don't you go talk to her?" David set his food down before saying, "I've already spoken with her today, and besides, she has a job to do, and It would be unprofessional to distract her." His father groaned, as if the air had been let out of his balloon, "Sounds like you've already got it figured out." David didn't respond but finished his food.

The day ended better than he remembered, and they left an hour before the park closed. After getting home, David helped his brother unpack the car and was outside rinsing out the cooler when a familiar car parked across the street. Tiffany got out and shot a look at him before she went inside her house. After finishing up, he swallowed his pride and walked over. Before he could knock, she opened the door and stepped aside. David walked in without saying anything and went straight to the back door. She looked at him curiously at first before following him outside.

He sat down on the same chair as before and she sat next to him, handing him a cigarette. He looked at the brand in her hand, GPC. He laughed, "You know what GPC stands for?" She smiled before lighting her cigarette, "Generic Pussy Cigarettes." He sat back in the chair smiling, "Exactly." Decades before, she had asked him this exact question, but he didn't know the answer then. As they sat in the dark smoking, David looked away, "Thank you for today." She smiled and responded, "You can do better than that." He turned his head toward her. "You're right." She stood up, closing the distance and looked him in the eye. "Fine, Thank you…" She pressed her lips against his, cutting him off. She sat down, "You owe me that much." He didn't respond but smiled.

Chapter 5

A Neighbor's Advances

Summer ended and the next year was about to start. For David, school was a formality he simply had to endure, because anything beyond his current education had never truly provided any sort of benefit, yet he still excelled. This year was different because he already knew what he had to learn in school. His brother had got his first car. Even though it wasn't worth the money it cost to maintain it, it was all he had. Weeks turned into months and the Fall break was about to start. David remembered this time decades before, his father was angry, and he was forced to leave the house. Back then, he just walked to the railroad junction a mile away and followed the tracks for miles until it got late. This time, he was going to be proactive and simply left.

As he walked, he decided to walk toward the school, changing his route from the last time. As he approached the intersection, just before the self-storage facility, he saw a girl sitting outside on the curb of the street. "Can I sit down?" he asked. "I don't care." The two sat in silence for a few minutes before he pulled his cigarettes out of his pocket and lit one. "Do you live around here?" she asked. "No, but I'm avoiding a fight, so I went for a walk," he responded. "My sister's fighting with my mom, so I left. How old are you?" "I'll be sixteen in the Spring," he answered. "Then why are you smoking?" "Old habits," he said as he stomped out his cigarette. "I'm David." "Jennifer." "Starting Highschool next year?" "Yes, how did you know?" "Lucky guess."

David stood and waved goodbye as he left. Jennifer sat on the curb for a few more minutes, then stood up to go back inside. After David got back home, he didn't say a word and simply went to his room. He knew why his dad was angry, he had started drinking again and he and his mother were having a fight. He didn't bother to see Tiffany, because she was visiting her family.

During the short time between the Thanksgiving Holiday and Christmas break, David didn't go outside much; he didn't like the cold weather, so he opted to stay indoors. One early morning, during the holiday break, there was a knock on his door. He got up and opened the door, "Tiffany, what are you doing here?" She was wearing a heavy coat and light blue jeans. "Can I come in?" Not wanting to be rude, he let her in and gestured to the couch. "Can I get you some-thing to drink?" "No, I won't be here long. I just came to ask for your help." He was surprised, she seldom asked for his help directly, so he was curious.

"What can I help you with?" he asked. "I want you to help me make Christmas cookies." He immediately thought about those romcom stories he used to listen to on the internet. For Tiffany, this was an opportunity to have a home date, but for David, this was an opportunity to teach her his notorious oatmeal cookie recipe. His parents were at work and the house was clean, so he saw no reason why he had to stay home. He told his brother where he was going and got dressed, making sure he shut the door. After getting dressed, the two went to the grocery store to buy more ingredients.

David was a no-nonsense kind of shopper, so the experience was more mechanical than social, frustrating Tiffany. After returning with the ingredients, the two began to prepare the cookie dough. Something could be said about making cookies with your crush, versus making cookies with a methodical and skilled baker, it wasn't fun at all. The kitchen turned into a cookie production factory, cleanliness and efficiency were not sacrificed for the sake of enjoyment. Tiffany was frustrated even more, but she was also impressed with his skill and proficiency. After the cookies were finished, David brought out a small plate of cookies.

After taking a bite of a cookie, she turned to David, "Do you ever stop and just relax?" David looked at her before responding, "I am relaxed." She set her cookie down and sighed deeply. "I wanted to spend time with you, not make enough cookies for a church picnic." David chuckled, "I guess I see your point. Is there anything you would like to do? I mean, I did kind of ruin your morning." "It's not ruined, it's just not what I expected. Although I will say, I'm not surprised." "So, you're okay?" "Yes, but that doesn't mean you don't owe me." "Oh?" "Yes, I want you to watch a movie with me." "Sure, we can do that, but what would you like to watch?" He asked. "No, I want you to pick a movie." He panicked, he couldn't remember what movies were popular at this time and using Google as a cheat wouldn't be possible.

David thought, "My movies or yours?" he asked. "Yours." She answered. He nodded and ran home to look through his parents' video library. A few minutes later, he returned with a VHS tape and put it in the VCR. He made coffee and brought two cups, sitting on the couch. Tiffany was elated, she ran to her room, bringing back a blanket. David could see her blush from one ear to the other. Poor thing, she probably had no idea what movie he picked. Meanwhile, she was lost in her own world, coffee, cookies and a movie under a blanket. David sat on the couch with the remote, as she pulled the coffee table close and set up the couch with drinks and snacks within reach.

David picked a war movie from the 80's and the two began watching. He didn't want to show his true age by commenting, so he was just going to enjoy the movie. Meanwhile, Tiffany wasted no time in closing the gap between them. Initially, she only sat next to him, but every time she sat up to get a cookie, put her cup down, or go to the bathroom, she got closer and closer. By the middle of the movie, she was in shorts and a t-shirt, with her legs on top of his. She grabbed his hand and wouldn't let go, holding it in her lap. He knew what she was doing, but didn't point it out. Eventually the movie ended, and she had pulled him almost completely on top of her.

The next movie on the tape was about to start and David started to get up, but he was pulled back. "The movie's over," he said, as if she had forgotten. "No, let's watch the next one too. It's still early and besides, what else are you going to do?" "Fine, we'll watch the next one, but after that, I need to go home." She smiled, "Okay, last one." This time, she didn't even watch the movie. He watched the movie, even though he didn't particularly like it, but he knew she wasn't interested in the movie either. David felt her pulling him in, if he wasn't aware of the optics, he would have had her moaning his name hours ago, but outwardly, he was still a young teenager, and he didn't want her to resent him. "Tiffany, it's not a good idea for us to start this." She pretended not to listen, pressing her face against his. "Tiffany!" She let out a deep breath. "I know, I know, but what if this is supposed to happen?" David couldn't answer such an absurd question, especially since his own life was so unnatural. She didn't fuss, but he let her kiss him on the cheek. They cleaned up the living room and he helped her pack the cookies. After he finished, he went home, thinking about how complicated his life could get.

The holidays ended, and school started again. This time, he was taking Drivers Education, and he would use his free period to get his driving time in. Because of his experience driving, this was merely a formality, and he would be able to get his license without any issues, not having to rely on his brother or others to get to work when he turns 16. Late one afternoon, David sat at the back of the band building, where his old friends would often play wallball, using tennis balls from the tennis court. Tiffany approached him and stood right in front of him. "Hey!" she called to him. "Hey Tiffany, what are you doing here?" "I heard you got your permit?" "I did, so?" he responded without looking up. "I want to take you to lunch." He let out a sigh, "Only seniors can leave school grounds for lunch, how am I supposed to get back in?" "We just won't come back," she said as she smiled.

David closed his book and looked Tiffany in the eye. "What are you scheming?" "Nothing, but we don't see each other much anymore and I wanted to help you practice driving." "You're lying." He let out a deep breath, "Are you sure you want to start this?" "Yes." Tiffany lowered herself in front of David, looking up at him, trying to keep her eyes fixed on him. "Fine, let's go." David took her keys and grabbed her hand, walking around the outside of the building until they reached the front. He held her left hand, pulling her along as she followed behind to his right. As he reached her car, he unlocked her door and opened it. After closing the door with her inside, he opened the driver-side door and buckled in. Starting the car, he waited a moment and turned toward her. "Where do you want to go?" "I don't know, I didn't think you'd come." "Fine by me."

He pulled the car out of the parking lot and immediately left campus. The roads felt smaller than he remembered yet still invoked a feeling of familiarity. He knew where he was going, yet didn't say a word. "You're a good driver, but that doesn't surprise me." "Why doesn't that surprise you?" "It's just that, between the two of us, I feel like the immature one." "I see, that's because you are." Tiffany scoffed and punched David on the shoulder playfully. Several minutes passed and they pulled into the parking lot of a Korean restaurant, no bigger than a convenience store. "Is this place any good?" "No idea, let's go."

They entered the restaurant and were immediately met by the attendant. "Dine in or take out?" she asked. "Dining in," he responded. As the attendant walked, menus in hand to the table, David grabbed Tiffany's hand and led her to the table, seating her facing him. After leaving the menus, she took their drink order. Tiffany opened the menu, looking confused at the selection. "What is this? I've never been to a Chinese restaurant like this." He corrected her, "It's Korean, and don't worry about the menu."

Tiffany continued to look at the menu with confused amazement, there wasn't a single picture, how was she supposed to know what to eat. Momentarily, the waitress brought their drinks and asked, "Good afternoon, are you ready to order?" "Yes, Bibimbap with beef and Osam Bulgogi," he said, handing the menus to the waitress. "Do you eat a lot of Korean food?" she asked, amazed at his confidence. "I haven't in a while." "Did your parents bring you?" "No, I went with a friend long ago." Tiffany pondered at David's words, he was honest, but how was he so familiar? The two sat quietly for several minutes before the silence broke. "When are you going to tell me about your books?" "You're still on that?" "Well yeah, there's something off about you and the more I think about it, the more I think the answer is in those books you keep." "Well, you aren't completely wrong."

The food arrived and they enjoyed their meal together. Tiffany had never eaten Korean food, and David seemed all too familiar with it. After the bill came, David handed the folder to Tiffany, who looked confused. "This was your idea, plus I don't have a job." "Fine, I guess you're right." She took the bill in a huff and placed a twenty-dollar bill in the bifold. David stood and prepared to leave.

Tiffany followed and they both went back to the car. After they got back on the road, David seemed to be driving with purpose. "Where are we going now?" "Well, we can't go home now, and going back to school is out of the question." Tiffany smiled nervously, she hadn't planned this far ahead, and David had taken the lead, so she was just along for the ride. "Have you made plans for after high school yet?" he asked. "Yes, I was going to take some classes locally and then probably transfer to a university." "Well, that sounds modest."

David didn't say anything, but he knew she was going to leave after high school, the lease on her mother's house was going to expire and they would be moving somewhere else, but he never knew where. They pulled into a parking space at an empty park and turned off the car. Tiffany looked around, the cold air had cast a fog over the playground equipment and the grass was still wet. "What are we doing here?" she asked. "Where else? Besides, I can show you my notebooks if you want." "Really!" Her eyes lighting up, "Yes, but I can only show you, don't ask me to explain anything about what is written." "Okay, I won't."

He reached down to grab his notebook. The edges were boxed and the pages wrinkled from so much writing. He handed the book to Tiffany, who seemed almost scared to open it. After taking a deep breath, she opened the book, and her eyebrow immediately curled up. Confused, she flipped back and forth, looking through the pages, growing more frustrated. "What the hell is this, I can't read anything in this book!" "I know, nobody can." "So, you've just been drawing stupid symbols all throughout this book for no reason whatsoever?" "Not exactly, I know everything that's written here, but I can't let anyone read it, so I made a code to encrypt it." "You're a freak, you know that right?" "Yeah probably." "How did you come up with this, is there a key to translate it?" "Yeah, I once took a class that required us to take notes, and if our notes were ever stolen, we would fail the class." "What kind of class was it?" "I can't tell you; it's in the book." "So, this book is full of secrets you can't share with anyone?" "Yes, exactly." "It looks prettier, the more you look at it. How does it work?" "Well, the characters are a mix of three types of script, the language is a mixture of three languages and the text direction is written from top to bottom." "Do you have to know these languages to be able to read it?" "It would certainly help." "You're a super kind of freak." Handing the book back, she announced, "I'm driving back, so change seats with me." The command hung in the air, a subtle power play that both exhilarated and unnerved her. She wanted to be in control, but also desperately wanted to relinquish it, to see how far he'd let her go.

As David opened the car door, Tiffany deliberately took her time unfolding from the passenger seat, stretching languidly, drawing out the moment. She could feel David's gaze on her, and a shiver of anticipation traced its way down her spine. After she slid out, David quickly moved to take her place, but Tiffany stopped him from shutting the door, a mischievous glint in her eyes. Taking advantage of his momentary confusion, she climbed into his lap, closing the door behind her with a soft click.

"You know, it's probably very difficult to drive from this seat," he said, his voice a dry whisper. She could feel the heat radiating from his thighs, a primal awareness pulsing between them. "Shut up," she muttered, but there was a tremor in her voice that betrayed her composure.

She wrapped her hands around his neck, sitting on her legs, straddling his lap. She felt the muscles in his shoulders tense and relax as he struggled to control his reaction. Rather than fight, he just waited, a quiet stillness radiating from him that both frustrated and intrigued her. Her body danced slowly, subtly in front of him, as she pressed her torso against his. She could feel the rapid beat of his heart beneath her own. For several minutes, neither spoke, the only sound the soft rasp of their breathing in the confined space. The air grew thick with unspoken desire.

Tiffany reached down near the door and pulled the lever that dropped the passenger seat back to the lowest position, creating a more intimate space. David wasn't surprised; he had been following her moves the entire time, but he wasn't about to make anything easy for her. The windows were completely fogged over, a hazy screen obscuring them from the outside world. It felt like they were in their own bubble.

Tiffany's head rested against David's chest, her hair tickling his skin. She traced patterns on his chest with her fingertips, little finger people exploring the landscape of his body. She turned her head upward, pushing her face toward his, her breath warm against his skin. He could smell the faint sweetness of her lip gloss. But as her face reached his, he turned away, a deliberate act of resistance. She didn't stop. She pressed her lips against the side of his jaw, breathing slowly into his ear, sending a jolt of electricity through him. As she moved down his neck, she coiled her body slightly, dragging a teasing finger down his chest in the process, following the line of his sternum. Just after she reached his collar bone, she sat up, never breaking her gaze. Her eyes were dark and intense, questioning, challenging. He still hadn't turned back to look at her, his jaw tight.

She removed her hoodie, the soft fleece sliding over her bare arms. Then, with a smooth, practiced movement, she pulled her shirt off over her head, tossing it carelessly into the driver's seat. The air in the car suddenly felt cooler against her skin. David finally looked up at her, his expression unreadable. "What are you trying to do?" he asked, his voice low and demeaning.

She smiled, a slow, seductive curve of her lips. "Trying to start something. Look, I know you said we're too young, but just let me have this." The words were a plea, laced with a hint of desperation. She wanted him to want her, to lose control with her. David didn't say another word. The silence stretched, thick with tension. He just watched to see how far she would take things, testing her boundaries, testing himself.

She reached back, unclasping her bra with practiced ease. She pulled her arms through the straps, then dropped the lacy garment onto the driver's seat. He was impressed by her confidence, by the deliberate sensuality of her movements. Her skin had gone pale after being out of the sun for so long, yet her tone seemed uniform, even across her shoulders. Her breasts, a firm c-cup, were topped with light pink nipples, about the size of a quarter each. Her nipples, which were initially sunk in a bit from the cool air, began to pop out, hardening in the close, humid atmosphere of the car.

She pushed her fingers under his shirt, sliding them up his chest, the cool touch of her skin sending shivers down his spine. She continued upward, pushing her hands up toward his head, tangling her fingers in his hair. She pulled his shirt off over his head and threw it in the pile on the driver's seat. As she reached down to grab his belt buckle, the anticipation was almost unbearable. He grabbed her wrist, his grip firm but not rough, shaking his head slightly.

She let go, putting her hands down on each side of his neck, her fingers lightly tracing the line of his jaw. Like a snake, she slid her body close to his, the soft friction of her skin against his igniting a fire within him. She dragged her tongue along his torso, from his navel to his sternum, a slow, deliberate caress that made him tremble. After stopping at his neck, she kissed the underside of his chin and rested her body against his. The weight of her, the heat of her skin, was almost too much to bear. He reached out to grab her hoodie, pulling it around both of their bodies, finding a strange comfort and protection in the soft fabric. He allowed her this moment, this stolen intimacy, but he knew he couldn't let it go any further.

"Wake up!" She jolted awake, disoriented, her cheeks flushed. She hadn't realized they had fallen asleep, locked in their embrace. The air in the car was stale and heavy with the scent of sweat and unspoken desires. Both quickly got dressed, their movements clumsy and awkward. She slid into the driver's seat, avoiding his gaze. After turning on the car, the clock on the radio read 3:10 PM. They had slept for nearly three hours. Driving home, neither said a word the entire way. The silence was heavy with the weight of what had almost happened, with the confusion and vulnerability they both felt. Twenty minutes later, they arrived. Thankfully, no one had come home yet. David grabbed his stuff, his face still flushed, and thanked her for the ride home before hurrying away, eager to escape the suffocating atmosphere of the car.

Tiffany sat in the driver's seat, slumped forward, holding her face in her hands for several minutes. The leather of the steering wheel felt clammy beneath her palms. Just how far was she willing to go? Her friends talked about sex like it was a normal, everyday part of their relationships, but her and David weren't even a couple. They were…what were they? She felt a wave of shame wash over her, a deep-seated discomfort with her own thoughts and feelings. After all, he was so much younger than her. Was she being predatory? Was she taking advantage of his inexperience? However, when they were together, her body seemed to surrender to him completely, and she felt like a little girl around him, vulnerable and yearning for something she couldn't quite define.

Why wouldn't he take advantage of her, it's not like guys his age weren't having sex, it just wasn't common in their circle. She thought a long time about the situation between the two of them, replaying every touch, every glance. Perhaps he was afraid, or she hadn't convinced him enough that it was okay to cross that line? Or perhaps, deep down, he knew her better than she knew herself, and he was protecting her from something she wasn't ready for. The thought both relieved and frustrated her. The road ahead felt uncertain, and she had no idea where it would lead.

Chapter 6

No Longer a Person

Spring had come and the weather warmed up. Of course, David went with his brother to work and applied for a job while he was there. As expected, he was hired merely two weeks after his sixteenth birthday. He saved half of every paycheck, something he neglected before, but wasn't going to neglect this time. He wasn't going to find a golden ticket, and his knowledge of the future wasn't going to yield some miraculous wealth, so he had to plan the best he could. His biggest priority was to save his children, and if things changed too much, he might not be able to.

A month before school ended, he was leaving his Geometry class, the last class of the day, when he was jump scared by a tall blonde standing outside of his classroom door. As he turned down the hallway to drop off his books in his locker, she followed. "Do you work tonight?" she asked. "No, I'm off today and Sunday." "Good, can I take you home?" He stopped at his locker and began putting his binder and textbook inside, leaving nothing but his notebook in hand. "Why do you want to take me home?" he asked. She reached out and grabbed his arm before answering, "Because I'll be going to college next year, and I'm moving with my friend early this summer to our new apartment. So, I won't be able to see you for a while." David resisted slightly. "Look, I don't think I can do this with you." "Why, is it because of the age difference? Is it because I'm going away to college? What is it that you have such a problem with?" She didn't seem upset or frustrated but concerned. At this point, they were both the same height, so the other students watching looked on with envy, rather than surprise. After all, David was quite well known amongst the other students and faculty.

David grabbed her by the hand and began walking her through the school, to the parking lot. "I'll explain why, but there are some things I can't tell you." "Okay." she said cheerfully. He wasn't sure if her sudden cheerful attitude was because he was going to answer her question, or because he was holding her by the hand. Truthfully, he didn't care, he simply wanted to get away from listening ears. They got in her car, and she drove home, engaging in small talk along the way. She was going to school several hours away but wouldn't be leaving the state. When asked about his plans, he simply avoided the question.

Upon arriving at her house, her heart began to race. Unsurprisingly, his was as well. Even though he put up a very stoic front, he actually found her quite attractive and endearing, but he knew who the mother of his children had to be, and what kind of woman would accept this? He didn't want to endure such heartbreak again, so he had to guard his heart, otherwise, he wouldn't have the courage to do what had to be done. She walked to her door, and he followed closely behind, waiting for her to invite him in before entering. As he sat on the couch, she put her stuff down and sat next to him.

"Who wants to go first?" he asked. "I'll go first," she said abruptly, as if she had been holding it in. "I appreciate you being the mature one of the two of us, but sometimes, I just want to have fun. I know there's more to it than just our age, don't ask me how I know, because it's hard to explain. It just feels like you're protecting me from you." "That's not exactly the case, but you're not that far off." He took a deep breath before continuing, "I know relationships are hard. Everyone has to compromise on something and eventually, someone ends up getting hurt. There are things I have to do, and I can't take anyone with me." "What kind of things?" "I can't tell you that, because if I do, I might not be able to do it. Anyway, I have to stick with this, and I can't allow anyone to derail my plans, not even you." "Well, is there something wrong with having someone to support you with your plans?" "Not at all, but could you ask someone to sacrifice everything, just to follow you, to trust you so completely? What do I even know, I'm only sixteen years old, what if I'm wrong?"

Tiffany's face suddenly became serious, he was right. Whether or not she agreed with his reasoning, he had obviously considered her future. It didn't matter what his plans were, he felt like asking her to follow him would be akin to giving up her own future, simply for his sake. "I understand what you're saying, but you're making assumptions about my feelings. Hypothetically, what if I did want to follow you?" "Then I would still have to tell you no, I have to do this on my own, it's a matter of life and death." She was relieved by his response but still confused by its context. "Is this going to go on forever, will it ever end?" "No, it won't go on forever." She jumped to her feet, excitedly, "Good, then it's settled." He was surprised by her sudden movement; she seemed hopeful, and he wasn't prepared for what came next.

She grabbed her bag and headed toward her room, "Come here really quick, I want to show you something before you go home." He hesitated before standing up, shrugging his shoulders, he walked down the hall toward her room. "What is it you wanted to show me?" he asked as he walked through the door. The door closed behind him, and she stood in front of it blocking his way. "You know you can't stop me from leaving." She approached him quickly, wrapping her arms around his torso. "Tiffany?" "I know." He didn't bother saying anything further. As she held him close, she ran her fingertips down his back as she mumbled, "I'm going to miss you when you're gone, but please don't forget about me." He let out a deep breath as he smiled, "I won't."

She pulled her head back and kissed him softly on the mouth, holding her lips in place as she teased the opening of his lips with her tongue. He only held out for a few seconds before reciprocating. As their tongues pressed together, she let out a deep breath, as if she had been holding it in, just as he took a deep breath, she could feel the pull. She giggled. "What is it?" She smiled while looking into his eyes, "You took my breath away." He rolled his eyes playfully, just before she locked her lips onto his again.

Tiffany took several small steps forward, a playful dance mirroring the growing tension between them, as he retreated in kind, each movement deliberate and teasing. The distance between them dissolved completely as they tumbled back onto her bed, the soft landing a stark contrast to the sudden spike in their heart rates. Her breath hitched, escaping in short, heavy pants, each exhale a testament to the rising desire. Her kisses were fervent, bordering on possessive, her tongue tracing the outline of his mouth, a gentle nip at his lip sending shivers down his spine.

He shifted back slightly, granting her unspoken permission to take control. With a newfound confidence, she straddled him on the edge of the bed, her thighs pressing against his. In a swift, fluid motion, she pulled her shirt over her head, tossing it carelessly aside. She leaned down, her bare breasts pressing against his clothed chest, the friction amplifying the heat that already simmered beneath their skin. Her kisses deepened, each one a silent plea for more. In the space between breaths, his hand reached up, his fingers deftly unclasping her bra.

The sudden release of tension caused her to recoil slightly, her hands instinctively crossing over her chest, a playful feigning of modesty in her eyes. "What, now you're shy?" he asked, the question rhetorical, a smirk playing on his lips. A coquettish smile bloomed on her face, and without a word, she tossed her bra aside, embracing the moment.

He sat up, deepening the connection as she wrapped her ankles around his waist. Her arms encircled his head, pulling his face into the soft valley between her breasts. As his tongue danced around the sensitive tips of her nipples, a low moan escaped her lips, her grip tightening, her hips instinctively arching towards him. He could feel the building tension in her body, an electric current that pulsed through her with each tantalizing caress. He deliberately prolonged the moment, savoring her anticipation. With a renewed urgency, she reached down and ripped his shirt over his head, casting it aside with the same abandon she had shown her own clothes. She pushed him back onto the bed, her movements now imbued with a palpable hunger. She climbed on top of him, her legs straddling his, her body molding against his. Her kisses trailed from his chin, up his neck, finally reaching the sensitive skin behind his ear, where she whispered, her voice husky with desire, "I want to do it with you."

He almost chuckled at her determined attempt to seize control, but her naiveté was endearing, evident in her words and the slightly clumsy urgency of her actions. He knew he couldn't take the lead; this moment needed to be hers, a true expression of her own desire. He pulled her close, his hand gently cradling the back of her neck as the other slid down her ribs, igniting a trail of fire in its wake. He kissed her deeply, passionately, guiding her gently to her side, laying her on the bed next to him. Her hands, emboldened by the shared intimacy, slid down his chest and rested on his belt line, her fingers tentatively exploring the contours of his body. His hand cupped her breast, his thumb teasing her nipple, while the other glided across her abdomen, a symphony of touch designed to heighten her arousal. She trembled slightly, a small shiver of anticipation running through her as she tentatively slid her fingers behind the waist seam of his pants, her fingertips tracing the top of the fastener. He didn't stop, didn't slow down, letting her explore at her own pace.

With a determined focus, she unfastened and unzipped his pants, her fingers fumbling slightly, betraying her inexperience. As she reached inside his underwear, the sheer size of his arousal made her pause. A moment of stunned silence passed before she looked him directly in the eye, a slow smile spreading across her face. He raised an eyebrow, a silent question hanging in the air. "Yup," he confirmed, a playful glint in his eye. She rolled onto her back, a playful display of confidence, and removed her own pants, her cute cotton panties now plainly visible as she lifted her hips into the air. She turned her attention back to him, her eyes expectant, waiting for him to reciprocate. "I'm not taking them off," he said, subtly shifting the responsibility back to her. She let out a frustrated little huff and rolled over to face his feet. In a swift, decisive move, she grabbed the waistband of his pants from both sides and pushed them down his legs, earning herself an unexpected smack in the face in the process. He chuckled, unable to contain his amusement at the comical turn of events, which only made her chuckle in a kind of resigned embarrassment.

His pants bunched up around his calves, hindering her progress. He lifted his legs, giving her the necessary leverage to finally wrestle the fabric over his feet. Finally free, she collapsed back onto him, draping one leg over his hip as she playfully traced patterns on his chest with her fingers. It was obvious she was nervous, yearning for him to take the lead, yet determined to remain in control. "Are you nervous?" he asked, breaking the silence. "Aren't you?" she countered, her voice a mix of defiance and vulnerability. "No, not really, but that's probably because I was born middle aged," he teased. She choked, unable to suppress a burst of laughter. "Then I guess you're going to have to teach me," she conceded, her eyes shining with a mixture of excitement and apprehension. He cupped her face in his hands and kissed her deeply, a comforting reassurance that dissolved her remaining anxieties, before gently pulling her underneath himself, ready to guide her through the uncharted territories of pleasure.

The air crackled with anticipation. He positioned himself between her legs, the gentle pressure of his body against hers sending a fresh wave of shivers through her. He paused, seeking confirmation in her eyes, a silent question: "Are you sure?" Her answering gaze was unwavering, filled with a raw desire that mirrored his own carefully controlled passion.

He kissed her again, a slow, deliberate exploration of her mouth that left her breathless and clinging to him. He shifted slightly, his hand tracing the delicate curve of her hip before gently guiding her legs higher, opening her to him. Her breath hitched as she felt the first tentative brush of his arousal against her entrance.

He could feel her tension, the almost imperceptible tremor in her thighs. He knew this moment was crucial, a delicate balance between fulfilling her desire and respecting her inexperience. He leaned down, whispering against her ear, "Relax, Tiffany. Just breathe."

He kissed her again, a deep, languid kiss designed to soothe her anxieties and ignite her passion. As her muscles began to loosen, he nudged her gently, testing her readiness. She met his gaze, her eyes wide with a mixture of apprehension and anticipation.

He pushed forward, slowly, deliberately, giving her time to adjust, to acclimate to the feeling of him inside her. He watched her face, searching for any sign of discomfort. Her expression was tight, her breath coming in short, shallow gasps.

He paused again, hovering just inside, giving her a moment to adjust. "Is it okay?" he whispered, his voice laced with concern. She nodded, her eyes squeezed shut, a single tear escaping and tracing a path down her temple.

He kissed it away, his touch gentle and reassuring. Slowly, he began to move, a slow, rhythmic dance that built in intensity with each passing moment. He watched her face as pleasure slowly replaced the initial discomfort, her eyes opening, her lips parting in a silent moan.

He continued to move, his pace gradually increasing, until she was arching beneath him, her hands clutching at his back, her breath coming in ragged gasps. He could feel her building towards the edge, her body trembling with anticipation.

He whispered words of encouragement, guiding her, urging her to let go. And then, she did. Her body convulsed around him, a series of intense shudders that sent a wave of pleasure washing over him. He held her tight, riding out the storm with her, until the tremors subsided, and she was left gasping for breath, her body limp and relaxed beneath him.

He collapsed beside her, his own breath ragged, his heart pounding in his chest. He turned to her, his eyes filled with tenderness. "Are you okay?" he asked again, his voice hoarse. She turned to him, a lazy smile spreading across her face. "More than okay," she whispered, her voice filled with contentment. "More than okay." And in that moment, lying naked and intertwined in the aftermath of their passion, David knew that he had made the right decision.

After more than half an hour, they both laid together in her bed. She rested her head on his chest, and he held her in his arm, dragging his fingers down her body. "I like you," she said softly. "I know," he responded. Propping herself up on her arm, she turned to face him. "When you get done doing what you have to do, will you come back for me?" He turned his head toward her, pausing for a moment before answering. "Only on one condition. You must yield to me completely." "Like a slave?" He smiled, "You remembered what I told you." "Yes, but I still don't know what that means." He sat up, keeping her bed sheet wrapped around their legs. "You can't question anything I do, and you have to trust me completely. If you think that there is ever going to be any doubt in your mind, then you should probably try to forget me. Because, when the time comes, you will belong completely to me. Not my partner, but my property."

She thought hard for a moment. "I'm assuming that your reasons are in that book of yours?" He nodded his head. "That's what I figured, so I may never know why." She looked down, as if in deep contemplation. "Just because I can't tell you now, doesn't mean I'd never tell you, but if you knew my reasons, you might agree for the wrong reason." "Is it worth it?" "Yes, but you have to give me something first." "My freedom?" David shook his head, "No, your submission." She leaned down to kiss him. "I need to get dressed, and I have to wash my sheets." "You can use baking soda and water to wash out blood stains." She blushed before responding, "Okay." He got dressed and left shortly after. At home, he took medicine for his headache, something he assumed was caused by his unique condition. Anytime his actions changed his former past, in a way that directly affected his current memory, he would get a migraine. So, he dare not try to change the course of anything significant.

In the weeks that followed, Tiffany waited in front of David's house nearly every morning to bring him to school, not that he minded, after all, her car was much nicer than his brother's. They talked about the time they spent together over the past few years, but they never talked about that day, and every time they passed each other in school, they would exchange knowing glances. With his new job, he was gone most nights throughout the week, so he stopped going to her house, which made these mornings much more significant. "David." "Yes?" "I want to spend time with you alone again." "Well, if you can get out early enough during final exams, it might be possible." She looked at him, "I only have to take one exam, what about you?" "I'm exempt from all of the exams." She shook her head, "Of course you are."

David didn't even bother going to school on exam day, so later in the morning, when Tiffany got home, he simply went over. After she let him into the house, she sat down, unsure of how to start. David looked toward the hallway and told her to make some drinks. "What are you going to do?" she asked. He looked back and said, "Don't question me." He walked to her room and left her in the kitchen. She wasn't sure what to expect, but she wasn't about to back out now. She walked into her room carrying two cups of coffee, David was sitting on her bed holding a shirt in his hand. "I didn't know what to make, so I just made coffee." "This isn't a test, you know I like coffee, so you did good. You're going to wear this shirt for the rest of the day." He lifted the shirt in his hand, but before she could grab it, he stood up. "Turn around." She set the coffee on the dresser and turned her back to him.

He leaned down and removed her shoes and socks, then stood up and reached around her waist, unfastening her pants. She only moved enough to help him as he undressed her. After he lifted off her shirt, he traced his fingers down her arms, as she lowered them. He unclasped her bra from behind and slipped the straps off her shoulders. "Turn around." She turned around, not saying a word. He held the shirt behind her, holding it open as she slipped her arms through. As he buttoned her up, she trembled. "Before you find out what it feels like to be mine, you need to learn to trust me." She nodded her head. "Don't be afraid to speak, I like the sound of your voice." She smiled. For the next hour, the two talked about simple things, sitting together on the bed while drinking their coffee.

After they were long done with their drinks, David pulled Tiffany into his lap. A shiver ran through her as he kissed the sensitive skin of her neck, pulling her tightly against him. They stayed locked in that embrace for a long while, the air thick with anticipation, before her hands began to explore him through his clothes, a silent invitation. He stood up, a playful glint in his eyes, and began to undress, starting with his socks, then his shirt, pants, and underwear, each article of clothing discarded with deliberate slowness.

As he approached her, Tiffany's fingers trembled as she began to unbutton her shirt, her gaze locked on his. He reached out, gripping her thighs firmly, and lifted her effortlessly, carrying her to the head of the bed before gently setting her down. He lifted her feet, slowly slipping her underwear off, the touch sending a jolt of electricity through her. He started by exploring the inside of her thighs with slow, deliberate licks, his tongue tracing a path higher and higher until her legs reflexively closed against his head.

He reached up and held her knees down, intensifying the sensation, pushing her further and further to the edge. He drank her in, his focus absolute, as she spiraled into a frenzy of orgasms, her breath coming in ragged gasps, her body slick with sweat and her own release. After a short pause to catch her breath, he sat up, his eyes burning with desire, and reached out his hand. She sat up, resting her chin in his palm, as he cupped the back of her head with his other hand, guiding her towards him just before sliding his cock into her mouth. Slowly at first, he guided her, allowing her to adjust to the unfamiliar sensation. Tiffany's desire urged her to take more, but her body wasn't quite ready, so she kept her mouth open, fighting to keep her teeth as far apart as possible as David plunged in and out.

The intensity of his attention, the feeling of being so utterly consumed by him, made her wet and responsive.

Instinctively, she reached down, her fingers tracing the swollen curves of her labia as he continued to thrust deeply. She closed her lips tightly around him, moaning audibly as she began to tremble again, her body consumed by another wave of pleasure. He released her and sat down, pulling her onto his lap, so they were facing each other. She could feel him pressing against her, the smooth length of his shaft gliding against her clitoris with each movement. She arched her hips, desperate to capture the tantalizing tip each time she thrust forward. Finally, she lifted her hips high enough, and the tip slid down, pressing intimately against her as she slowly pushed forward, taking him inside.

The two fucked with primal abandon for another half an hour, their movements a dance of pure instinct, before she collapsed, breathless and exhausted. But this was not the end. For the next four hours, they continued their passionate exploration, taking short breaks between each intense encounter. Tiffany had completely exhausted herself, her muscles aching, and even the thought of walking to the bathroom seemed like an impossible task. David, on the other hand, seemed to be fueled by an endless well of energy. They had both showered and meticulously cleaned her room before her friend Sandra arrived with her car, the remnants of their passionate encounter fading into a sweet, lingering memory.

David was making the bed when the doorbell rang, so he rushed to open the door. Tiffany, refusing to stand up, yelled for her friend to come inside. Upon entering,

Sandra took a long look at David before turning her gaze to Tiffany. "You're a bad girl; you didn't tell me he was the guy you were talking about." Tiffany blushed before responding, "He's my neighbor and he's just helping me out." Sandra squinted her eyes, studying the both of them before turning to David, "So you're the helpful neighbor?" He nodded. "What are you helping with today?" David smiled at Tiffany before responding, "Fucking her brains out." Sandra nearly split her side laughing as Tiffany turned various shades of pink and red. "I fucking knew it!" The week after her graduation, she packed her things and prepared to leave with Sandra. Before leaving, she hugged David, whispering into his ear, "Don't forget about me."

During that summer, his ex-girlfriend Donna was hired at the same restaurant he worked. In his past life, this relationship became toxic shortly after the new year, ultimately forcing his parents to intervene. By the summer of the following year, he was forced to move out for going against their wishes, which is when he finally broke up with her, but her wrath and manipulation weren't something he could escape, after all, she was a woman and anytime they fought, he was automatically viewed as the aggressor. The following fall, he was expelled for attacking her, and later that spring, he was arrested for assault. Something he didn't have the experience or the money to fight in court, so he accepted the plea.

Chapter 7

Unreasonable Demands

When school started, he was on a new path, one without his ex-girlfriend. Rather than falling in with his brother or his old friends, he decided to make his own way, he sat quietly at a table by himself, reading and taking notes in his notebook. One morning, a familiar voice called his name. "David!" He looked up, "Jennifer, looks like you made it." "Yeah, why are you sitting by yourself?" "Well, my brother has his own group, and my friends don't get in till later, so…" "Where does your brother sit?" David pointed to the corner, where his brother and friends would gather every morning. Jennifer looked with a surprised expression. "That's who my sister used to hang out with." "Oh really?" feigning ignorance.

David knew exactly who Jennifer and her sister were, because after he was kicked out of his house, he lived with his brother's friend for a while, then stayed in Krystal's apartment when everyone moved. This is because Krystal was a part of his brother's friend group and Jennifer is Krystal's younger sister.

He had originally met Jennifer much later, toward the end of his senior year. "Well, you're new here, why don't you sit down. If you don't claim your territory now, you'll just end up attaching to a group you don't know."

"Really? Wait, what about my friends?" David smiled, "They can sit here too, the more the merrier."

David knew that if he didn't start his own group, he would be in the same position. This way, not only does he have the advantage, but he can also establish his dominion for the next two years. "Can I leave my bag here; I want to get something to eat." "Go ahead, I'll watch your stuff."

As she left, several students passed by the table, pushing chairs and shoving tables as they passed. David just shook his head, knowing this was a power play by another group trying to establish their own footing. As luck would have it, they sat at the table next to his. The group of five kids, obviously freshmen, wore their pants low and barked profanities at every opportunity. Jennifer returned, seeing the group out of the corner of her eye and pretending not to be bothered. "I'm back, thank you," he nodded, "You're welcome."

As Jennifer ate her breakfast, the group kept talking loudly, slapping the table and aggressively standing up, slamming their chairs into people, including Jennifer. She moved her chair to the side, but her actions didn't go unnoticed. Suddenly the topic of conversation changed to a loud discussion about David and Jennifer. Soon, their crude language and insults became aggravated when they started throwing trash and even reached for Jennifer's backpack, scraping their feet against it.

David became impatient and put down his book. Looking directly at the group, he said firmly. "If you five are so desperate to start trouble, why don't you go outside and start it there, nobody in here has the stomach or the patience for your bullshit." Of course they were offended, as if they had no idea that they themselves were offensive. Shooting back with insults, they dared him to repeat what he said. "You heard me, take your little show outside or shut up." David said firmly.

Three of the five stood up, inching to David, who was still seated. The cafeteria was starting to fill up, and the commotion attracted onlookers from every direction. A crowd started to form around the noise and spectators began to talk amongst themselves. "What are you doing? Sit your stupid ass down before you trip over your pants." David said, exasperated. He had dealt with these types of people before, and the reason you never see these types of people as an adult, is because they almost always end up on drugs, in jail or dead. When society collapsed, men that continued to bully others, were often dealt with ruthlessly.

David stood up and as he turned, his head jolted to the right with a flash of darkness, his left ear throbbing. To his right, one boy stepped forward, David kicked, stomping down on his abdomen as he dodged, grabbing the arm coming from his left, he pulled hard as he raised his elbow, striking the boy's face. As the boy on the right charged again, he rotated his hips, bringing his leg against his knee, followed by a haymaker. Returning to his left side, he caught another punch in his arm, pinning his wrist against his chest as he pushed forward, dropping his body down, dislocating all of the bones in the boys wrist. The third boy didn't move as the others backed off.

The clamoring only lasted for a brief moment, but the shouts brought the vice principal quickly. The fighting stopped and David sat down. Nobody asked questions and the five thugs were escorted to the principal's office. David's brother, who still sat in the corner, watched the entire event unfold, leaving his entire group in shock. He was aware of David's sudden change but had never seen him in a fight since then. Jennifer thanked him and started sitting right next to him from then on.

The morning went as usual and during second period, an office aide showed up to the classroom with a piece of paper in her hand. The teacher turned toward David, "David, you're wanted down in the principal's office." Without a word, David grabbed his stuff and promptly left the classroom, following the aide.

David entered without knocking and sat on one of the chairs in front of the secretary's desk. In less than a minute, the principal's door opened, and the resource officer waved him in. As he sat, the principal asked, "David, are you aware that the punishment for fighting is mandatory suspension?" David responded respectfully, "I am, but are you aware that assault with bodily injury is a misdemeanor and punishable by up to a year in jail plus fines and probation? After all, they threw the first punch."

The resource officer raised his eyebrows and looked at the principal, seemingly waiting for his response. "Are we going to have you back in this office again?" "Hopefully not for something like this, but you'll be the first to know." "You were hit first?" The resource officer asked. "Yes, he sucker punched me when I wasn't paying attention, I even told them several times to stop." "Are you injured?" "That depends on what your plan of action is for them." "They're going to be expelled for the rest of the semester, with the possibility to return next semester." The principal said as if asking a question. "Then I'm fine, nothing I can't handle. Can I go now?" The principal nodded, "You're free to go."

David nodded and left the principal's office. The rest of the day went without issue and the next day, several of Jennifer's friends started sitting at the table in the morning. After school that following Friday, Jennifer was waiting halfway between the north exit by the buses and the main entrance on the south side, when she saw David walking toward the north parking lot. She ran after him, hoping he would walk her home, as all her friends either took the bus or rode with a parent. Even though she never had any particular interest in him other than familiarity, the other morning had left an impression, and she now saw him as her white knight. "David!" waving to get his attention "David, wait up!"

David looked at her and even though he didn't say anything or stop, he did slow down, as if expecting her to catch up. "Are you headed home?" "Of course." "Can I walk with you?" "I'm not going to stop you." As Jennifer skipped through the parking lot, David suddenly stopped as Jennifer kept going. "Oh, you're not walking?" "Not as long as my car's here." With a look of defeat, Jennifer lowered her head, turning away to continue walking. "Hang on!" he called out. "Huh, what is it?" Suddenly perking up "If you want a ride, just ask, if you don't, just go; but don't start acting like I took away your favorite toy just because you found out I have a car. It's a bad habit to get into."

She was flustered, feeling attacked. Jennifer tried to find the words to express her frustration, but there was none, she had been found out and his aloof response to her childish behavior seemed to put her on edge. Despite this, Jennifer refused to respond, David had become a benefactor of sorts. "I didn't want to ask you for a ride, and besides, I only live a few blocks away." "I'm aware, but it cost me nothing to allow you to ride along, unless your family would have some problem with me taking you home." "They might, my mother won't let me do anything anymore, not since my sister got pregnant."

David didn't ask further, he put his bag in the trunk and sat in the driver's seat, starting the car. Jennifer climbed in the passenger seat and tucked her bag between her legs. David left the parking lot without saying a word. After a short drive, he pulled up near the storage facility, a landmark he recognized nearly a year prior. "Which house is yours?" Jennifer pointed out a small white house with green trim, two houses away from the entrance of the storage facility. David turned around, parking in front of the white and green house on the corner.

As Jennifer was gathering her possessions, David left the car and walked toward the front door. Jennifer watched him, concerned about his intentions. He knocked firmly and waited with his hands in his pockets. As the door opened, he noticed the familiar sight of an older woman, several years older than his own mother. "Good afternoon, my name is David, and I brought your daughter home from school." "Thank you." she said dismissively. "You don't have to bring her home, we live really close to the school."

She was not disrespectful, but her intentions were obvious, to demotivate him from pursuing her. She was even planning to address this issue with her daughter later. However, David knew her apprehension, she was already dealing with the aftermath of her oldest daughter's rebellious behavior and would do everything she could to keep her youngest daughter away from any boy that cast any desire toward her. David, knowing this, did not back down. Jennifer was not a stunning girl yet, but he knew she would quickly mature, and she might make a promising companion in the future. "May I come in and talk, I would like to discuss your daughter now while we have the opportunity."

Struck by his straightforward approach, she had no justifiable reason to refuse his request. "Don't mind the mess, you can sit wherever you want." "Thank you." As he sat down on the couch, avoiding the pile of laundry on the other side. "My name is Laura, thank you for bringing her home. So, what is it you wanted to say?" "I am an acquaintance of your daughter from school, she might have mentioned me, and I felt it would be respectful to make contact with you directly, rather than relying on rumors and hearsay."

Laura was shocked, but pensive at his statement. She was prepared to reject him before he could make any declarations, but he was quicker with his words. Jennifer had quietly entered the house, sneaking off into her room. She sat quietly on her bed, trying to listen to the conversation. "You also believe your daughter is too young to be in a relationship, and I'm not here to try and change that, but I am here, However, understanding this isn't enough to keep her from pursuing a relationship with people her age." "You don't have to tell me; I'm her mother after all and I know what's best for her." Her attitude turning defensive, "I'm not here to tell you what to think, I'm only here to make myself known, what you do with that information is completely up to you."

Laura had nothing to say. She knew he was right but couldn't argue with his words. He had indeed come to talk with her, something most boys his age would avoid. David stood, straightening his clothes as he stood. "I have to work this evening, so I won't keep you. Before I go, in case you have some reason to use it, can I give you my parent's phone number?" "Sure." Laura had no intention of calling, thinking this was a one-time attempt to curry favor. Still, he wrote his number down and handed it to her. Then he walked out the door, promptly getting into his car and driving home.

Jennifer came out of her room, waiting for her mother to scold her. "You've only been as school for a few days and already brought a boy home." Jennifer didn't respond. "He's a smooth talker, but that doesn't mean he can be trusted." Jennifer clenched her fist before responding, "You don't even know him and you already hate him?" Laura sighed and rubbed her head, "Don't you think it's a coincidence that this boy would suddenly offer to bring you home? How did you two even meet?"

Jennifer sat down, pressing her fingers together in her lap. "I met him last year when you and sis were fighting. He was avoiding a fight too and we just happened to meet outside." Laura raised her eyebrows but wasn't convinced. "You remember Krystal's friends, the ones that play Dungeons and Dragons all the time?" Laura nodded, "Yes, what about them?" "Well, David's older brother is one of them, but we didn't know at first. Plus, he was looking out for me when a bunch of guys tried to start trouble the other day." Laura considered Jennifer's words. "Maybe I'll call his parents after all."

A few months later, while sitting in his World History class, a note was put onto his desk. He turned to look and the boy sitting behind on his left just shook his head. He pocketed the note until after class and went back to trying to use mental powers to make his history teacher pee her pants, but with no success. After class, he read the note and promptly tore it up and dropped it into the garbage.

After school, he was met by Jennifer in the hallway by his locker. She didn't bother to hide her attachment to him and would even wait for him in the hallway, when their classes were close together. "Are you going home now?" she asked. "Not yet, I have something I need to take care of." "Oh, can I come with you?" "Sure, just keep your distance and wait where I tell you." "Uh, okay."

She was unsure of his response but wasn't about to question him. He walked briskly through the hallway, past the cafeteria and around the corner toward the art department. "Wait here," he said, pointing at the corner, before the hallway's intersection. She obeyed without hesitation.

He entered the classroom and there was a girl he hadn't seen or thought about in a very long time. Summer, a girl he once thought was pretty in the fourth grade, was finishing up a painting assignment for art class. He never took painting, and he only remembered having one class with her in High School, and that was a government class. Summer hadn't spoken to him since the fifth grade and honestly hadn't considered her much since starting middle school, yet here she was.

"Hello Summer, you wanted to see me? He asked. "Yes, I'm sorry for asking you here like this, but I didn't know how you would react if I asked you in person. After all, we haven't talked in a long time." "Don't worry about it, I don't think anyone our age has it all together, so there's no reason to take it personally." She smiled, comforted by his words. She bit her lip and began fidgeting with the brush in her hand as he looked toward her painting. "I didn't know you liked to paint, it's odd we didn't end up in art class together." Her face lit up, "Yes, I remembered you like art. Have you taken any classes in High School?" "I have. I took drawing last year; I'm taking sculpting this year and I'm taking the advanced class next year." "Oh, I should have figured." She spoke with her head down.

He observed her posture and demeanor, looking back at the door, then back at her painting. Obviously, she wasn't there to catch up, or to discuss art. "Why did you want to see me? I thought you were doing your own thing?" "I, I am, but it's not that much. I'm not in any programs, and I still don't have a lot of friends." David remembered her getting bullied by another girl in their class when they were children. He had tried to stand up for her, but she didn't want his help, even yelling at him, so he just let it go, and they hadn't spoken since.

Perhaps this is why she didn't have very many friends. He honestly didn't know. But since then, he had started hanging around different groups and their social circles simply never crossed, so he never bothered to find out. However, this time, everything was different. He kept to himself, but the teachers and school staff seemed to like him. He wasn't in any programs or clubs, yet he was popular. He didn't take any advanced core classes, but he got exceptional test scores. He didn't have a girlfriend, but she hears what other girls say about him in secret.

"Do you have any plans after High School? "Yes, as a matter of fact I do." Holding up his notebook. "I even have them written down here." "Can I see? I'm curious to see what kind of plans take up a whole notebook." "Nobody can read this book except for me." She pouted. "Well, you obviously aren't trying to get into college, because you aren't taking the right classes, so what will you do?" "I'm going to enlist in the Army, try to have children, and retire early. Plus, college won't do me any good, besides, it wouldn't make a difference." "Children? Are you going to get married? You have a girlfriend?" He shook his head, "No, I don't."

She was confused, how would he have children without a wife or girlfriend? Did he have a girlfriend before? Was it the little blonde girl that keeps following him around? "Look, it's been fun catching up, but I have things I need to do, and I don't like wasting my time, so if you'll excuse me, I need to go." He turned to leave but was suddenly grabbed by the hem of his shirt. "Wait, don't go yet. I wanted to ask you something, but I've been too nervous. Will you give me just another minute?" He stopped, pausing for a moment before responding, "Okay, say what you want, I don't dislike you, even though we haven't spoken in a while, so you don't have to worry about being hurt." She took a deep breath. "Would you ever consider having a girlfriend?" "If it was someone like you?" he asked. "Yes, someone like me." She held her breath, her heart pounding on her ribcage, as if it were about to explode. "No," he said coldly. "Why not?" she asked.

He walked right up to her and grabbed her arms, inches from her face, "Summer, I want you to listen carefully to what I'm about to say. I am not going to offer myself to anyone as a prize to be won, or as a punk to be taken advantage of. I don't belong to anyone, not even you. However, I am not cruel. If you get on your knees and forfeit your body to me, I will take care of you. It's that simple. However, if you bring poison and chaos into my life, I will put you down, like an animal." Her cheeks blushed red from ear to ear, and she was on the verge of tears, but nothing in her mind could be made into words, she was completely dumbfounded. He let her go and left the classroom without looking back. Jennifer was standing right outside of the door when he came out, but she didn't say anything.

David was getting a headache, rubbing his eyes as they left the school. As the two made it into the parking lot, she finally spoke. "Did you mean what you said?" He nodded his head. As they approached his car, she hesitated. His words stirred in her mind, and she almost kept walking, unsure if he even wanted her hanging around him. "Get in the car." Her heart nearly burst from her chest at his words.

From the time she sat down, until the time they pulled up to her house, she couldn't take her eyes off him.

He just told her to get in the car, like he was her father, picking her up from school. Did he see her as a child? Why did she feel so hot? Did he feel responsible for her, or was she just following him around like a puppy? Suddenly, a thought flashed in her mind, making her blush. After they arrived, she got out of the car without saying a word, running straight to her room and throwing herself onto her bed.

Chapter 8

It's Called Jealousy

Jennifer's attitude began to change after that day. Originally, her high school debut was supposed to be all about her independence from her older sister's shadow. However, she didn't expect to find such comfort in someone else's. David never treated her like a woman, which frustrated her, but she wasn't about to complain, especially the way he responded to girls his own age. At least she was with him, even if he only saw her as a little girl. On her birthday, she went with her friends to the mall and with possessive determination, she was going to make him see her. She visited the boutique first, eyeballing the accessories. As she looked, his words kept repeating in her mind, "Forfeit your body to me", "Like an animal." She recalled her own thoughts from that day as well. Would he take care of her like a puppy?

She found it, a token of her acceptance. With this, she would establish her place by his side. After leaving the boutique, she went to the salon to finish her look. Her friends, waiting in the food court, gasped as she approached. The first thing they noticed was her hair, changed from a shoulder-length chop to a short bob. Her short hair sculpted her neck and shoulders, which revealed the other change, Jennifer was wearing a velvet choker around her neck. The two boys in her group began to comment, was she goth now? Is she going to start wearing stockings and lace? Her three girlfriends immediately zoomed in on the choker. "Did he make you buy that?" one asked. "No, I wanted to myself," she responded.

Her reception at school was about the same, several classmates asked about her new look, but Jennifer thought discussing it was akin to showing off, and she didn't want to cause trouble for David, so she kept her answers short. David's treatment of her hadn't changed initially, but he did notice her studying more, making healthier lunch choices and acting more reserved in crowds. When he asked her, she assured him that she was perfectly fine and simply wanted him to be proud of her. After some time, school was returning after the holidays and the old Jennifer seemed to have been forgotten.

In the five months since school started, Jennifer matured quickly, gaining recognition from her classmates, but her attention remained solely on David. Every time school let out, she rushed to his locker, waiting for him to arrive. Unlike Tiffany, she never asked about his work or his hobbies. She believed that as long as she didn't push him, he would always have a place for her next to him, a point of pride that she carried with her.

One afternoon, as she waited for him, several sophomore boys began to approach her. One even daring to propose, "Hey, I see you here all the time and I was wondering if you wanted to walk home together." She shook her head and looked away, not saying a word. The boys blocked her in on three sides, as the boy made another attempt to be the main character in her high school romance. Had it not been for his friends pressuring him, he might have given up, but his pride overpowered his common sense. "I'm trying to be nice to you, you don't have to be such a bitch." Bam! His head slammed against the locker and suddenly everyone stopped moving. David looked down at the boy on the floor, then back at Jennifer. "Let's go," he said without looking at the other two. She stepped over the boy's legs and wrapped her arm around David's as they walked away.

As they walked to his car, she let go of his arm but remained right by his side. He stood nearly six inches taller than her, a towering difference that filled her with pride and joy as she walked in his shadow. She skipped to the other side and sat in the passenger seat, waiting for David to get in. He didn't mention the incident at the locker, but Jennifer was obviously buzzing from the incident. As he sat down, he took a deep breath, "Go ahead." She smiled and kissed him on the cheek before settling back into her seat, "Thank you for saving me, again." He smiled before starting the car. On the way to her house, she bounced in her seat as they listened to music all the way there. Before she got out, she leaned over and kissed him hard on the lips, lingering for just a moment before she ran inside.

As the school year came to an end, David's father moved back home, and his older brother had gone to the

Army recruiter to enlist. David continued his cultivation and went to work. He signed up for Mixed Martial Arts classes to take during the summer and continued to write in his notebook.

The school year ended, and summer was finally here. His brother left shortly after graduation and David got his own room. Laura, Jennifer's mother, had warmed up to David, accepting him and even trusting him with her daughter's safety, for the time being. Meanwhile, Jennifer had become more besotted by him. During the day, he took various martial arts classes, further cultivating his body and abilities. At night, he would work, continuing to save money. Donna, his ex-girlfriend from his past life, quit her job after a new store manager took over and without David's support, she had no reason to stay, he never even gave her a chance to be friends.

One June weekend, he had agreed to meet Jennifer at her house, taking her to the water park, something he had done with Donna in his previous life. When he arrived late in the morning, she was waiting for him in front of her house, wearing a blue swimsuit under a t-shirt and shorts. David walked past her, taking her hand as he went straight to the door. He greeted Laura, having a quick discussion about their plans before preparing to leave again. He knew she was protective, fearing her youngest daughter might follow the same path as her sister, who had gotten pregnant at a young age and was living in a woman's home due to the abuse suffered at the hands of the baby's father.

As they departed, Jennifer sat next to him in the car, proudly displaying her body to him like a trophy for his admiration, but David didn't comment. She wasn't disappointed by his silence, because she was aware of his attitude and just allowing her to be near him was a victory in and of itself. She was perfectly content being his pet, after all, when was a pet mistreated by such a capable master. The water park was nearly an hour's drive away and she remained hyper fixated on his actions, the way he handled his car, the way he spoke with such discernment, the intimidating yet disarming look in his deep blue eyes, even his physique. She began to writhe in her seat, clenching her hands between her thighs.

"Don't think I haven't noticed the choker you started wearing, is that something you decided on your own, or did your friends help you make that decision?" She was snapped out of her fantasy, stammering with her words, "No-no, I got this for myself, it wasn't something I was talked in to." He had some idea why she wore it, but he wanted to hear her explanation. "Is that for my benefit?" She was shocked into silence by his completely accurate assessment. "Uh, yes," she mumbled, nodding her head. "After that girl Summer confessed to you, I didn't want to be left behind, I can see how pretty she is, plus she's your age, while I'm much younger and I look like this." "Yes, I've known her for quite some time, I even had a little crush on her when I was in elementary school, but that was a very long time ago." Jennifer retorted, "That was only like seven years ago, does that feeling just go away?" David chuckled, "It feels more like half a century." Jennifer's heart surged at the sound of his laugh, completely unaware of what he actually said.

As they arrived at the water park, Jennifer ducked her head to look out the window. "Have you been here before?" he asked. "Yes, but it's been a long time," she responded. "The main pool used to be much deeper, but they had to fill it in a few years ago," he said as they parked. They both walked to the entrance and David paid for their bracelets. After entering the park, David pointed toward the changing rooms and told her, "Take off your shorts and t-shirt in there, you'll want to change out of your swimsuit when we leave." "Ok." Jennifer blushed, she hadn't brought any underwear, and she was wearing a white t-shirt. David, on the other hand, was prepared.

After changing, they both met between the main pool and the leisure river, where there were many lounge chairs. There, David told Jennifer to turn around and began applying sunblock. How is he so shameless? Jennifer's heart was racing the entire time. When he was done, he handed her the sunblock and turned his back to her. As she glared at his broad shoulders, the freckles on his back made her body quiver. He wasn't some flawless character from a story, he was imperfect, a normal person with flaws and problems, just like the rest of us. "Uh, Jennifer?" She hadn't even started putting on his sunblock, when she heard her name, she was resting her cheek against his back, her hands gripping his shoulders. "Oh, sorry. I lost my train of thought," she said quietly.

They spent time swimming and floating in the tubes down the river, occasionally taking a ride down the water slides. After several hours, David was getting bored, and Jennifer was fixated on closing the gap between them. He decided to use the large pool to swim laps back and forth, while she was trying to coax him back to the river. In the end, she hung on to the side, watching him swim.

The pool was 130 feet wide and 200 feet long, a bit larger than an Olympic sized pool, and David had swum its length about twelve times before it dawned on her that he was some kind of freak in the water. On his return for the thirteenth run, he never came up out of the water. The reflection of the sunlight made it difficult to see underneath, especially at her angle, and she began to panic. But before she got out of the pool to try and look for him, he surfaced just past her on the other side. "David!" she lunged at him, grabbing him tightly. "You scared the shit out of me!" He didn't fight her, after all, this wasn't the first time he had scared someone in the water. David was a skilled swimmer, and he could hold his breath for quite a long time, so this wasn't a big deal for him, but it seemed to stir something in her.

Jennifer grabbed him tightly, pressing her lips against his. A loud whistle broke the tension. "You two knock that off!" A lifeguard had called them out on their little make out session, and Jennifer felt embarrassed. "I'm sorry for doing that," she said, turning away from him. He could tell she was embarrassed, and didn't want to make her feel awkward. "You didn't do anything wrong, so you shouldn't feel embarrassed." She smiled, stepping toward him. "Let's go get something to eat, I'm hungry." "Alright," he agreed.

They both got changed and prepared to leave. Jennifer was self-conscious in her clothes and David didn't seem to notice. "What would you like to eat?" he asked. "I don't know, but let's get take-out, I think I'm too under dressed to go inside." "It's the summer, I don't think you're under dressed." She leaned close to him, "I'm not wearing any underwear," she whispered. The information hit him like the plot line of an explicit joke. "Oh, then I guess we'll just find someplace to get carry-out."

Suddenly, she began to panic. "Shit shit shit!" Jennifer was looking around frantically, unrolling her towel and even digging through her bag. "What's wrong, did you forget something?" Tears welled up in her eyes and she nodded her head. "I lost my choker, I have to find it!" David didn't respond immediately but thought for a moment, "Why is that choker so important, didn't you just buy it from the store?" "Yes, but I don't want to be seen without it," she hung her head.

David picked up their food and stopped at a picnic area near the lake to eat. If he was going to address the issue, this might be a good time. "What happens if others see you without it, wouldn't that be normal?" "I don't want to be normal, I want to be yours." He pondered before responding, "What if you change your mind, or what if I decide that I would rather have somebody else?" "I don't care! I'm not going to change my mind." He could see that she was prepared to die on this hill. "Alright, if that's what you truly want, I won't stop you." She bit her quivering lip, "Does that mean I can be your girlfriend?" He sighed softly, "No, it doesn't." "Okay, I understand." She sat back in her seat, lifting her shirt off her body.

"What are you doing?" David exclaimed. "If I can't be your girlfriend, then I can at least be your pet." What kind of books has this girl been reading? Clearly, she was serious. "Why are you taking your shirt off?" She got up, leaning close to him before answering, "Will you make your dog wear clothes in such hot weather, Isn't that cruel?" She licked the side of his neck, up to his ear. It took every ounce of self-control he had to keep himself from ravaging her right there in the car. He pushed her back down into her seat by her shoulders, "Sit." "Woof!" He almost lost his composure.

He took her home and prepared to walk her to the door. As she prepared to go inside, she leaned forward and kissed him. I hope she isn't going to be this affectionate at school, because that could be a problem. After she went inside, he turned to go back to his car. "David!" she called out. He turned back, "What is it?" "My mother went out for a bit, can you wait with me until she gets home?" Oh boy, this sounds like a setup. Shaking his head, he started toward the front door, "Alright."

No sooner than he sat down, she pounced on him. "Jennifer, I…" She cut him off, kissing him again. "I want you so badly. I want you to ruin my body and make me yours." Clearly this girl was in heat, but what could he do? He wasn't about to fuck her in her mother's living room. Plus, what if she came home? And besides, this might just be an infatuation. "I won't do that; you're only 15 and you might regret it later." She didn't back off, removing her clothes right there at his feet, "Please fuck me, I want you to be my first!" She was persistent. Taking down his shorts, she grabbed his cock and without hesitation, buried it deep in her mouth, as if it were on fire. Her method was crude and sloppy, obviously she had absolutely no real experience, but her desperation to have him inside of her kept him hard, despite her clumsiness.

Her left hand held him like a vice, as her right hand, buried knuckle deep inside of herself, gripped her clitoris like a wet bowling ball. David, keenly aware of the situation, could smell her, she was masturbating in front of him, and he had to act quickly, before she went further. She stood up, straddling his knees as she approached. Her body dripped on his legs and her skin began to glisten from sweat seeping from her pores. She sat on his bare lap, pushing her hips tightly against him, "I want you inside of me." She moaned in his ear. As she grinded her labia against the girth of his shaft, a car pulled into the driveway.

Quickly, she grabbed her clothes and took off toward her room. David pulled up his shorts and stayed seated. As Laura entered the house, she greeted him. "How was the waterpark?" she asked. "It was hot, but I think she had fun. Oh, and I got her some food on the way home." "Oh, that's very nice of you, thank you." "You're welcome." Now that her mother was home, he decided that it was best to leave.

David arrived home and took a black ribbon from his mother's craft box, he crafted a small choker and set it aside. He was off today, so he stayed in his room, waiting for the night to pass. As he sat at his desk, he heard a knock at his door. "David, somebody at the door for you!" his father called out. He went to the front door and as his father stepped aside, he gasped. "Tiffany! What are you doing here? Tiffany smiled and pulled him outside. "Sandra's visiting her parents for the summer, and I wanted to see you." David smiled as Tiffany held him tightly. "You've gotten taller," she said quietly. He looked at her, indeed, he was nearly an inch and a half taller than her. "I still have a few more to go," he said, almost reassuringly.

David invited her inside for a bit and she followed. As she went into his room, she looked around. "I don't know what I expected to see, but somehow this doesn't surprise me." His room was organized, various non-fiction books on his bookshelf with a small stack of composition notebooks. "I didn't know you had so many," she exclaimed. "I run out of space." She smiled and sat down on his bed. "How have you been, any closer to conquering the world?" He chuckled, "No, not yet."

As he sat down, she noticed the ribbon and the choker, sitting beside him. "What is that?" she pointed at the choker. He looked over and handed it to her. "This is a choker; someone I look after lost hers and I decided to make a new one." Tiffany held the choker in her hand, contemplating its significance." Without looking up, she asked, "What's her name?" "Jennifer," David responded without hesitation. Tiffany sat in silence for a moment, deciding if she should leave or stay, but David didn't say anything. "What was it you promised me?" Tiffany asked, on the verge of tears. "I promised to never forget you." She nodded her head and put the choker back on the desk.

Tiffany stood up, ready to leave when he called out, "Tiffany, what did I tell you?" She stopped, not looking at him, she responded quietly, "I have to trust you completely." She stood for a few moments before turning around. David was still sitting on his chair; she knew he wouldn't chase her if she left. She approached him, knelt down and looked up at his face. "I need one too." He was almost shocked, he fully expected her to leave without turning back. Placing his hand on her head, he agreed, "I know just the color." She smiled before lowering her head onto his lap.

He pat her shoulder, gesturing her to stand up. David walked to the kitchen and filled a cup with water. "Would you like a drink?" She shook her head, turning to go back into his room. He shrugged and followed her in. She was sitting on the edge of the bed, hands wedged between her knees as he sat down at his desk. He finished his water and put his cup down, then she slid down to her knees right in front of him. Grabbing the hem of his shorts, she pulled them down to his ankles and grabbed his cock with her right hand. She placed his cock on her tongue and sucked on it three times, swirling her tongue around as it hardened in her mouth.

Pleased with her efforts, she kissed the tip and began devouring it like a melting popsicle. David didn't grab her head, nor did he stop her. After an exhausting few minutes, she swallowed every drop of cum he shot in her mouth, licking it clean before pulling up his shorts. "You went swimming today." He nodded, "Yes, at the waterpark." She sat on his lap, hanging her arms on his shoulders. "Did you fuck her yet?" "No, but she tried." Tiffany chuckled, "She should make you wait." David smiled, "Touche!" She kissed him before standing up, "I have to go, but I'll be here for two weeks. Make time for me, please." David agreed and she left.

Chapter 9

Decoding David

Several days later, David woke up early, he had promised Tiffany he would spend time with her and Jennifer was going to her grandparents' house for a month. Shortly after 9:00am, a car pulled in front of his house, and Tiffany knocked on the door. David opened the door and let her in. "How has college been?" He asked as he turned to pick up the shirt he was going to wear. Before she answered, she grabbed him from behind, turned him around and kissed him fiercely. "It's just more school," she answered. His younger brother was in a summer program, so he was home alone.

David wasn't about to break the house rules, so he quickly got dressed and prepared to leave. Tiffany followed him out, "Do you want to take your car?" David looked at her car, then back at his. "Get in," he gestured to his car. She smiled as she let his hand slide through her fingers while she walked toward the car. David opened the door and sat behind the wheel, as she buckled her seatbelt. "Big plans for today?" he asked. "I'll tell you when we get there," she smirked.

David pulled out of the driveway and got on the highway. As he drove, Tiffany kept her hand on his, even as he shifted gears. She smiled as she watched him drive, she never learned to drive a stick, but he did so like it was second nature. David drove for several hours out of town until he reached an overwatch just off an unfinished road. She looked around and was about to ask where they were when David got out of the car. Putting on her sunglasses, she got out and stood next to him. "What are we looking at?" she asked seriously. "David grabbed her hand and pointed toward a large opening down in the valley below the hills. "I'm going to buy that land and build a house."

Tiffany looked at the plot of land and turned to David, "How big is it?" "About 35 acres." Tiffany leaned against him as he rested against the hood. He wrapped his arm around her as she tilted her head to kiss him. "Are you sure you don't want any help?" He kept staring at the valley in the distance. "I might, but I can't trust anyone yet." She turned her body toward his and pushed herself into him. "Well, I'm completely yours if you can remember that." David smiled, "Remind me."

Tiffany didn't hold back, she started taking her clothes off right there in front of him, hanging them over the barbed wire fence. David removed his shirt and dropped his pants before turning her around toward the car. He grabbed her waist tightly as she reached down, guiding him inside of her. With her hands pressed firmly on the hood, he thrust his cock inside of her, gripping her hips firmly as she moaned unabashedly. He wasn't loving or gentle, as he shamelessly used her body as an object of sexual gratification, until her knees to give out. They decided to move their game into the car, as the afternoon sun would surely leave a mark. David climbed into the back seat and Tiffany mounted him, and for nearly an hour, they continued their activity until her legs felt like jelly and even the car's air conditioning didn't help.

Tiffany slept in the passenger seat while David drove back home. They arrived late in the afternoon and his parents were already home. He walked her to her car, and she kissed him again before leaving. He went into the house and made dinner before settling down for the night. The rest of the summer was busy, with his work, classes and his plans, until school started again.

David didn't pass up on the chance to take work Co-op classes again. Especially since that got him out of school early. He also decided that he was going to start picking Jennifer up in the morning, after all, he felt kind of responsible for her. Otherwise, he expected it to be an easy year. That is, until he got to his English class. "David!" He heard his name as soon as he walked in the door. "Summer, what the hell are you doing here?" This wasn't right, clearly, she had reorganized her schedule, because he didn't change anything with his. "What are you talking about, this is an English 4 class, not shop. Why would you be surprised to see me." David couldn't say, but he knew she had changed her schedule for a reason, but how did she figure his schedule out?

Of course, the games had begun; first it was the people in front of her, then the vent was right overhead, add a little bit of ass kissing and she ended up picking her own seat, right behind David. This girl was after something, but why did she have to play these games? Other than this, classes were relatively normal, only this time, he wasn't going to be kicked out of his house, so he could work on himself with his free time. Jennifer was no longer confined to the freshman wing of the school, so he saw her in the hallway more often than last year. David made her a choker, because she insisted that replacing it with something out of a boutique would water down its sentiment.

The school no longer separated lunch for the upper classmen and the lower classmen, which created its own problems, but with more seniors going off school grounds for lunch, the only ones affected by the crowding and long lines were the students. Unsurprisingly, Jennifer begged David to spend at least some time with her during lunch, which he didn't mind, as long as she controlled herself at school.

At the end of September, David entered the main hall, near the cafeteria and spotted Jennifer and Summer talking over by the snack bar. Was there going to be an argument? He had to find out. Summer saw him first, "David, over here!" He shook his head, "No shit, did you think I was coming here to get a personal pizza? What are you two conspiring about?" Jennifer looked at Summer, then back at David and smiled. "She was just asking about us. She wanted to know if we were dating." David nodded his head as he listened. "I was just curious, because we have a class together and I wanted us to be friends, but I didn't want to get in the way," Summer added.

David pinched his forehead, "What is the monthly subscription fee?" Summer looked puzzled, "the what?" "The monthly subscription fee for being friends. Do I have to buy gifts, do I have to fight your bullies, am I supposed to call you a certain number of times per week?" Summer's eyes started to turn red. "I don't understand." Her voice started to shake. David realized that he might have been too harsh. "Let's go somewhere else and talk." The three went to an open classroom and sat down.

"I'm sorry for being so harsh, but I don't value friendships the way you do. Every relationship that I've ever known has had some kind of exchange or agreement, even with my parents. You're either an accomplice, a colleague, a business partner, or a subscriber to some kind of service." Jennifer and Summer didn't interrupt, after all, nobody could get close to him on their own terms, it had to be on his. "I don't have friends, I never have, and I never will. Any partnership or agreement ends as soon as your function has ended. Otherwise, your friends become shareholders in your own life, and I'm not a publicly traded entity."

Jennifer didn't understand what that meant, but Summer understood completely. "Then how do you meet new people, if you don't want to make friends?" He thought for a moment, "You're asking me how I would eventually accept you?" Summer didn't realize when she asked her question, that it could be picked apart so easily. "Or how you and Jennifer ended up here?" "Uh-huh" David was not impressed with her deflection.

"Jennifer is like a puppy. She was nice when I met her, she follows me, she keeps me company, and she lets me pet her. After a while, I'll start to bring her food, maybe even a toy. Now I'm pretty sure she has an owner, so I can't legally take her home, but if I do, I'm going to put a collar on her and I'll even get her own little dog bed." Jennifer wore a grin from ear to ear, while Summer couldn't seem to grasp the content of his words. "So, you're calling women dogs?" she asked, testing his response. "No, I would never do that, it's just an analogy." "Oh, okay." "But that doesn't mean you don't want to be someone's pet, especially of you find the right master." David stood up, walking toward the door. "Come!" Jennifer jumped up and followed him out, as if by command. Summer's question was answered but was left with even more than before.

Summer never owned pets, so she had no frame of reference. Her exposure was limited to what she saw on TV and what she heard from others, but she wanted to understand his comparison. The next week, David was passed a note from behind, he recognized the handwriting. Not that he needed to, Summer sat right behind him.

I still don't understand the comparison between people and pets, but I want to, what can I do to learn more. Where do I start?   *-Summer*

David tore up the note and threw it in the trash on the way out of class, but as Summer left, he stopped her just outside the door. "Come to my house and I'll explain to you, how I take care of our dogs." Summer was surprised, she thought he was blowing her off after watching him tear up the letter. David picked her up from school later that afternoon and took her to her parents' house, she needed to ask permission before going somewhere else.

When they arrived at David's house, he explained the unique care that is required for taking care of specific dog breeds, their diet, their temperament, their strengths, and their weaknesses. He had Dachshunds, so he knew all about the breed. Summer observed and could tell they were well taken care of. Not just their needs, but the enjoyment and the attention they get as well.

Several days later, David took Summer for a long walk down several blocks, pointing out the different dogs. One such dog was obviously an outside dog but was confined to a small kennel in the back yard. It was obvious that many of these dogs were not taken care of in accordance with their breed, and several of them were neglected.

Summer finally understood the comparison. An animal can only be a pet, if it has a good master. Pets that are taken care of have long, healthy and meaningful lives. So, it's important for a master to adopt the right pet, just as it is important for a pet to tell their master what their needs are. Summer was more confident, but she wondered, was David a good master?

A few weeks later, David received a call at work, a new restaurant was opening in town, and he was being recruited. He remembered this from the past, only Donna wasn't here to criticize him. He accepted the job, especially since it was what he had done in the past and his current job was closing down in a month. The following week, he aced his interview and started his new job, this time, without the added headache. While training for his job, he met a familiar face, Sarah. It was Sarah's parents that introduced him to his future ex-wife, when things didn't work out with Sarah the following year.

Months had passed and the holidays were about to start. Everyone was getting two weeks off from school and Jennifer was already scheming, she had turned sixteen a month ago and she was finally allowed to get her driving permit, but her mother wouldn't pay for driver's ed until the last semester, which didn't start until the end of February. This was convenient for her, because David would be eighteen in the spring, and she was desperate to milk every opportunity to get him alone. Summer was no longer sharing a class with him, but he was expecting to see her in the spring for Government class. However, this didn't stop her from making up every excuse to talk to him when she could, usually under the guise of learning something new.

Thankfully, she had stopped trying to convince David to pursue traditional friendships and relationships but ended up taking a page out of Jennifer's book. She would often show up where he was, but dared not interfere with what he was doing, and because she learned where he lived, she also showed up at his house from time to time. David seldom turned her away, but somehow, always found a way to make her useful. He would assign her chores and make her take one of the dogs when they were being walked. Only when he had to go to work, or when she was there too long, did he send her home.

It didn't take long for her to figure him out, but she never saw him smile, and his bedroom looked like a tiny studio apartment. One day, while sitting in his room, she finally asked, "David?" "What is it, Summer?" "What happened to you?" David set his pen down, nobody had ever asked him this question before. "He turned around and looked right at her. Her heart began to pound in her chest, she had never seen him react so dynamically to a question before. "Why are you asking me this?" She thought for a moment before continuing, "You're a high school student, but you act like a combat veteran." He didn't say anything. "You don't play, you don't go out, you don't challenge yourself in school, but you punish yourself at home. So, what happened to you?"

David grabbed a stack of notebooks off his shelf and set them down next to Summer. "Everything is in there." She opened the first book and started flipping through the pages. "What is this? It looks like a foreign language, but I've never seen it before." David was impressed. "How did you know?" She kept looking, "Because there are a limited number of characters, and they all fall into a pattern like words." "Clever girl." "These are catalogues of everything I remember, this one is a list of plans that I have, and that one is the latest journal of everything that's happened this time."

She looked at the books, there were about nine in total, all of them filled. She picked up the first book and opened the first page. Everything was written from top to bottom, except for the upper margin. There were eight characters in sequence: an equal sign, a dot, another equal sign, the letter V, another dot, another equal sign, a hyphen, and a square.

Summer began to worry, either he was completely insane or he was onto something. She excused herself and went home. While she was there, she wrote down the code from memory and sat in her room. As she sat there, she tried to figure everything out, but how could she? He wasn't talking and what was with the secret codes? The more she thought about the problem, the more she thought about David. It was his personality, everything about him changed suddenly and yet it was still him. He struggled to pass before and now he gets straight A's and school is useless? He always had trouble making friends, but now he's popular and friends are pointless? And what kind of teenage boy doesn't want a girlfriend? It's like he's afraid of relationships, but he keeps Jennifer around.

As Summer ate dinner, she turned to her father and asked, "Dad, why would a man never want to get married?" Her father was shocked at her question. "Well, most men I know don't want to get married for a few reasons, either their ex-wife took everything they owned, or they have their own ambitions, and they think a woman will just get in the way." Summer lowered her head, she didn't want to ask the question again, so she let it go.

The next day, Summer told her dad she was going to her friend's house and went straight to David's. She knocked on the door and David let her in without a word. It was 10:00am on a Saturday and next week was the last week before Christmas break. David poured a second cup of coffee and put it in front of Summer. She looked at the coffee, wondering if it would be rude to refuse it. She thought she would try to talk to him, but she didn't know where to start, so she just watched him. He didn't speak, he didn't even act like she was there, other than handing her the coffee.

She set the coffee down on the table and sat down on the couch next to him, he was budgeting his finances in a ledger. Seriously, what teenager has a budget. "Are your parent's home?" she asked. "My father is on shift today, so he's not here and my mother is reading in her room." "Don't you have a brother?" He answered without looking up, "My older brother is gone, and my little brother is probably playing video games." "Is your older brother in college?" He shook his head, "No, he joined the Army." "Really? I thought about joining the reserves." David responded without thinking, "Good idea, you should pick a medical occupation."

Summer was taken aback; this is exactly what she was planning but hadn't told anyone. She was more determined than ever to figure out his secrets. "David, how old are you?" David thought for a moment before answering, "I'm seventeen years old." She leaned in, "Why did you have to think about it?" "Because it's a ridiculous question." She thought again, "I have one more question." David looked her in the eyes. "What happens in thirty-six years?" His heart sank, "How did you?" She pulled out a piece of paper with the code written on it.

"I memorized the code, because I thought it was significant." She held out the paper and began to explain, "You forget, we both shared a class with Nick, the boy from Taiwan, and you were so excited to learn Chinese numbers, plus you started carrying around that Arabic book at the end of fifth grade. I figured it had to be a date, so I spent the night figuring it out." David took a deep breath, "It's just a story, it's not real." Summer sighed, "You aren't being truthful. I knew something was wrong when I saw your room."

David took a deep breath, "I can't trust anyone." Summer scoot close to him and cupped his cheeks, "I think you're afraid that I'm either going to take everything from you or that I'll somehow slow you down, I promise that's not going to happen." David couldn't look away as she looked directly into his eyes and began to cry. She was startled by his response and waited for him to calm down, but he cried for several minutes before finally catching his breath.

"When I was thirteen, I had a dream about the world ending and I lost everyone in my life I ever cared about, my children, my parents, and my girlfriend. Since then, I've carried the trauma and memory of that dream, as if it were real." She could feel his pain but was almost relieved by his explanation. A dream was just a dream, but how could he remember it so vividly? "You don't have to carry this burden with you, it's just a dream, and life is real," she said reassuringly.

Chapter 10

The Birthday Present

The holiday break was over, and the senior class was buzzing about the end of the year. Several committees had stalls lining the main hall. The yearbook committee sold yearbooks, the prom committee sold tickets, job fairs and various representatives from local colleges handed out information pamphlets, and school clubs were recruiting new members for the next year. Of course, David wasn't interested in these things, but with Jennifer in tow, he approached the prom ticket counter.

"I'd like two tickets," he said nonchalantly. Jennifer was nearly jumping out of her skin. She looked up at him, "Am I even allowed to go to the senior prom?" David responded without looking, "Who said I'm taking you?" The student council rep selling the tickets immediately changed their posture and broke eye contact at the suddenly awkward situation in front of him. Jennifer pouted and lightly bit his arm. "Ouch, alright, alright. I was kidding." He handed over three twenty-dollar bills, a high cost for such an event. Jennifer jumped with excitement before suddenly stopping. "What about Summer?" David was confused, "What about her?" Jennifer looked at the ticket in her hand and said softly, "She won't have a date, and I think she wants to go with you." David shrugged it off, "If she wanted to go, she would have asked about it already."

Several weeks had passed and the new term had just started. Prom was three months away, but Summer hadn't come over to David's house since that day before the holiday break. David still picked up Jennifer on the way to school, and even though she was as feisty as ever in private, she maintained a reserved posture in public. Government was his second class for the day, after swimming, his third was Co-op.

As expected, Summer sat directly behind David, but this time, he sat toward the back of the class, unlike the English class he shared with her during the first term. David was writing in another notebook before class started as she looked over his shoulder. "What are you writing?" David answered without turning his head, "I'm writing down the answers for the assignments for the class, so I don't have to do them later." Summer was speechless, if he knew the assignments for the class then what he told her couldn't possibly be a dream. It's one thing to remember something from your past, but even a genius would find this degree of recollection impossible.

"So, you're just not going to do any work for the rest of the year?" she asked. David scoffed, "That would be a waste, I'll read the book too and probably just spend the rest of the time in my notebook." Summer understood his intent, If David had perfect memory recollection, then waiting for the assignments to be released would get boring. "How much do you remember from your dream?" Summer felt silly asking this question, because she didn't believe for one second that this was all from a dream. "Well, I remember everything perfectly, but the stuff I'm learning now, seem to fade like normal memories." She thought for a moment, "Is that why you write everything down now?" He nodded, "Yes."

She sat back, waiting for class as he continued writing. During the class, the teacher discussed the syllabus and before class ended, she assigned their first homework assignment, they were to read a portion of their textbook and answer the questions in the back of the chapter. Before class was dismissed, Summer tapped on David's shoulder, "Did you already finish this one?" He held open his notebook, showing his completed homework and closed it as he packed his things. She was stunned for a brief moment before shaking it off and catching up to him.

"David, wait up!" He stopped, "What is it, Summer?" "I want you to go to prom with me." He turned toward the direction of his next class before responding, "You know that I'm taking Jennifer, right?" She hung her head as she walked, "I figured you would, did you ask her to go?" He shook his head, "No, but I knew she wanted to go, plus, she probably won't go when she's a senior, so…" She smiled, "You really do take care of her, don't you." "I can't change my nature," he replied. Her mood suddenly shifted, "I'm going to go buy a ticket, what color dress should I wear?" David thought for a moment, "How about something yellow?" She chuckled, "Why not a sunflower dress?" He understood her comment, "No, but if you ask my opinion, you're going to get an honest answer, truthfully, I really don't give a shit what color dress you pick, as long as it's not purple but let me know what you decide." She smiled before leaving.

Jennifer waited for David near his locker before lunch; he didn't have any more classes, so he was done for the day, but he would sometimes stay during lunch. As he walked up, Jennifer asked, "Did she ask you yet?" "Ask me what?" "Did Summer ask you about prom?" He let out a sigh, "Yes she asked." "Is she going?" she asked excitedly. "You are way too excited about me taking her to prom," he scolded. "I like her, plus she isn't competing with me." David wasn't as surprised as he should have been by her response.

One weekend, David was at home, training in his back yard when his mother came out onto the back porch, "David, you have company!" "I'm coming!" he responded. David set two steel bars down against the wall of the house before going inside. As he opened the door, he saw Summer standing there. "Summer, why are you here today?" She didn't speak at first, lost in her words, she only looked at him in the doorway. David rolled his eyes and opened the door wider. "Come inside, when you figure out what to say, just let me know." She walked straight to his room, as David got a drink of water.

He stepped out of the kitchen, "Where did she go? His mother pointed toward the hallway, "Probably your room." He went to his room and saw Summer sitting on his bed. "I'm sorry for interrupting you today, I didn't know you were busy." He waved his hand, "It's okay, I could use a break anyway." She kept looking at his body as she spoke, but David didn't seem to notice. "So, what were you doing?" David smiled, he always liked explaining himself, "Come here, I'll show you." They both went into the back yard, and he picked up the two metal bars, about four feet long, each with grip tape wrapped around the ends.

He held the bars up, swinging them and moving them around, as if he were choreographing a dual saber sword fight. She was mildly impressed at first, but quickly realized that not only was he quick, but skilled as well. He set the bars down and wiped his hands. "That's really impressive," she commented. He didn't respond but looked away embarrassed. "Plus, they didn't touch once the entire time. How long have you been doing that?" He flinched, as if physically hit by the question. "Today? I don't know, only a couple of hours." She smiled as she reached her hand out to pick one up. "Fuck! How much does this thing weigh?" She strained as she lifted it. "Well, it's solid steel, so probably forty-six pounds."

She let out a deep breath as she lowered it to the ground. "No wonder you're in such good shape." She mumbled to herself. "Huh?" "Nothing, let's go inside." The two went inside and went to his room. "Why did you come here?" he asked. Rubbing the back of her neck, she responded quietly, "I was wondering if you would tutor me." He smiled, "Bullshit, that's not even a believable excuse." She huffed, "Maybe not to you, but it is for everyone else." David raised his eyebrows at the sudden realization, "Oh, I get it. Sure, I'll tutor you." He stood up suddenly and left his room. Summer didn't move. He opened his door and sat back down. Summer looked at his hands, then back at the door, "Where did you go?" she asked. "I told my mother that I was going to be tutoring you until finals." She smiled.

David and Summer sat in silence for a few minutes before he spoke, "Why do you want to go to prom with me?" She hesitated before answering, "Because I wanted you on my side." He sat back, "Explain." She took a deep breath, "I know you use to have a little crush on me, then I was mean to you, and you stopped talking to me. I honestly thought you hated me. Suddenly your name kept popping up and I started to notice you more. Sophomore year, that senior kept hanging around you, then last year Jennifer started clinging to you. Obviously, you have a thing for blondes, so I figured your crush made sense." David continued to listen as she spoke. "I know I didn't treat you fairly, and I wouldn't have been surprised if we never spoke again, but I always felt bad. You walked me home every day and I blew you off when I got scared, which wasn't your fault."

"So, you feel sorry for me?" David asked. "No, I wouldn't have the guts to talk to you if that was it. I just really want that time back." David leaned forward, "It's not your fault, I don't deal with rejection or abandonment well, in fact, I cope with abandonment by convincing myself that I hate the person, in order to deal with it." Summer held her breath. "Does that mean you hate me?" He shook his head, "No, I'm more self-aware now, I understand your position, plus, I wasn't always the easiest person to deal with." She lowered her head, "Is that what happened before?" "Before what?" "Before you woke up." David sat back in his chair, "It is, we never spoke again after elementary school."

Summer stood, then sat in David's lap, hanging her arms on his neck. "Don't, I'm all sweaty and I probably smell." She smiled flirtatiously, "Oh, I know." Looking him in the eye, she asked, "Did you have a girlfriend?" "Yes, but she was an evil bitch that ruined my life." She chuckled, "Did I have a boyfriend?" "You did, but I don't remember much about him." She raised her eyebrows, "What was he like?" He smiled before answering, "I know he was small and thin, even our government teacher made fun of him when he knew you two were dating." "Oh, I think I know who you're talking about."

Summer's face was inches away from David's when his mother called, "David, you got a Birthday card!" Summer got up quickly, straightening her clothes, "It's your birthday?" He shook his head, "Not for a few weeks." He left the room and quickly returned with a card in his hand. She noticed the handwriting and the red envelope, "Who's it from?" He turned the envelope to read the address information. "It's from Tiffany." Summer was confused, "Who's Tiffany?" David opened the envelope as he answered the question, "She use to be our neighbor, but she went to college year before last." "Does her parents still live here?" "No, she moved shortly after." Summer watched as he read the card, "Why would she send you a birthday card?" David put the card back in the envelope and placed it on his bookshelf. "We kind of have a thing." She gasped as she realized, "Tiffany is that senior, isn't she?!" He smiled, "You're smart."

David got ready to take a shower, so Summer went home. That night he had to work, so she had no reason to stay. Several days later, he had a day off and came back to school in the afternoon to take Jennifer home. After they arrived, he followed her to the door. "Good afternoon, Laura." "Good afternoon, David, what brings you here today?" David sat down before answering, "I'm taking Jennifer shopping to get a dress for the prom." Laura gasped, "What? She never said anything about going to prom!" David was shocked, "Jennifer!" he yelled. Laura laughed, "I'm just kidding, she told me all about it." David, still shaking from the ordeal, "I was going to tell you, but it just seemed too obvious, plus I'll be leaving next fall. "Oh dear, where are you going?" "I'm enlisting in the Army, and I'll start my training then." Laura nodded but had a look of worry on her face.

"Ready!" Jennifer declared, emerging from her bedroom, now clad in a stylish sundress, a stark contrast to the clothes she'd been wearing earlier. The change in attire hinted at the importance of their outing. "Alright, let's go," David said, pushing himself up from the couch. He grabbed his keys and headed for the door, Jennifer close behind. They walked in comfortable silence to the car, the afternoon sun warming their faces. As Jennifer buckled her seatbelt, a soft giggle escaped her lips. David, however, remained quiet, his expression unreadable.

As they sat in the car, Jennifer's gaze kept drifting towards him, a coquettish glint in her eyes. There was a playful energy about her, a hint of anticipation that David couldn't quite decipher. "What is it? I feel like you're going to burn a hole through me with your stare," he finally said, a slight smile playing on his lips. She smiled back, her eyes sparkling. "I was just wondering... what kind of dress is Summer going to wear to prom?" He looked at her, puzzled. "I don't know. Why does it matter?"

She shrugged, trying to appear nonchalant. "I don't know, I just thought it would be fun if we matched. You know, a girl-friend thing." David chuckled. "No, it wouldn't. You need to pick a dress that makes you stand out, something unique. You don't want to blend in with the crowd." She smiled, seemingly satisfied with his answer, and leaned back in her seat. The air crackled with unspoken feelings, a subtle dance of attraction and playful rivalry.

The two arrived at the mall and parked on the North side, conveniently close to the department store. The sprawling shopping center buzzed with activity, a kaleidoscope of shoppers and brightly lit displays. For nearly two hours, they wandered through the dress sections, their footsteps echoing on the polished floors. Jennifer meticulously surveyed various styles, colors, and fabrics, seeking the perfect outfit. David patiently trailed behind, offering occasional opinions and acting as a sounding board for her indecision.

Finally, after much deliberation, they settled on a stunning blue dress with delicate thin straps and a flirty, full skirt. It was simple yet elegant, and it perfectly complemented Jennifer's figure. "Are you going to get something for prom?" she asked, carefully holding the box containing her coveted dress. "No, I already have something prepared," he answered mysteriously, a hint of a smile playing on his lips.

As they got ready to leave, Jennifer handed David a folded stack of money. "What's this for?" he asked, surprised, as he examined the bills. "It's from my mom, for my dress. She wanted to contribute," she explained. He shook his head. "Fair enough. I appreciate it." David paid for the dress and a few carefully selected accessories – a delicate silver necklace and a pair of strappy sandals – before turning to Jennifer. "Is there anything else you want? It's still pretty early." Jennifer's cheeks flushed a light pink as she lowered her head, a shy smile gracing her lips. "Yes, but it's not here." David nodded, intrigued by her cryptic response. "Okay, let's go then."

After they got back in the car, David turned to Jennifer, curiosity piqued. "What is it you wanted to get?" She was fidgeting with her fingers, a telltale sign of nervousness or excitement. "It's a birthday present for you," she finally confessed, her voice barely above a whisper, "but I needed to get it before your birthday, so you wouldn't suspect anything." He smiled, touched by her thoughtfulness. "Just tell me where to go, and I won't ask any more questions." Her face lit up, her shyness momentarily forgotten. "Okay! Let's go next door to Walmart first!"

He drove to Walmart without saying another word, respecting her request for secrecy. After they arrived, she practically leaped out of the car and ran inside, disappearing into the front door. David waited patiently inside the car, watching the bustling activity around him. After about ten minutes, he saw her running back towards the car, clutching a small plastic bag in her hand, her cheeks flushed and her eyes sparkling. "Did you get what you wanted?" he asked, amused by her enthusiasm. "Yes!" she said, slightly out of breath. "It was the last one!" "Where to now?" he asked, starting the engine.

She thought for a moment, her brow furrowed in concentration. "Actually... you can just take me home now. I'm not feeling very well," she said, her voice sounding slightly strained. David was mildly concerned. "Are you sure? You seemed fine just a few minutes ago." "Yeah, I think I'm just a little tired," she replied, avoiding his gaze. He didn't press her further, taking her straight home. After a brief conversation with her mother, he left, feeling vaguely unsettled by the sudden turn of events.

The next morning, before he left for school, his phone rang. He glanced at the caller ID and saw it was Jennifer's house. "Hello?" he answered. "David, this is Laura, Jennifer's mama. I'm just calling to let you know that she's sick and won't be going to school today." He paused, surprised by the news. "I'm sorry to hear that. I had no idea, but thank you for letting me know." "You're welcome, dear. Goodbye." "Bye." After he hung up the phone, he grabbed his keys and drove to school, a nagging feeling of unease lingering in his mind.

Halfway through the morning, he felt a nudge on his ribcage. He turned to see Summer, her eyes mischievous. "What is it, Summer?" he whispered, trying to maintain the teacher's attention. She leaned closer and whispered back, "Where's Jennifer?" "She's at home sick today," he replied, a touch of concern in his voice. "Are you going to check on her later?" she asked, her voice laced with a hint of playful challenge. He thought for a moment. "Yes, I probably should."

A few minutes later, he felt another poke at his ribs. "Jesus, what is it, Summer?" he whispered, his patience wearing thin. She leaned in again and whispered, "I got my dress! It's silver colored, and it sparkles like crazy!" "Cool," he replied, trying to sound interested.

David felt another poke against his ribs, this time he turned around, a flash of irritation in his eyes. "Fuck, what do you want now!?" Summer, seemingly unfazed by his outburst, leaned in and kissed him quickly on the lips as he turned his head. "I got dibs," she whispered, a knowing smirk on her face. He turned back toward the front, bewildered and slightly flustered. What the hell does that even mean?

After school was out, driven by a mixture of concern and curiosity, he went to Jennifer's house. Her mother usually worked early in the morning until about 3:00 pm, so she wasn't home. That's why David thought it would be a good time to check on her. However, when he got there, she didn't seem sick at all. "Jennifer, why did you stay home if you weren't sick?" he asked, a hint of accusation in his voice.

She bounced out of her room, her eyes sparkling with excitement. "I was so nervous that I felt sick!" "Nervous about what?" he asked, his brow furrowed in confusion. "I was worried you wouldn't like your present!" she exclaimed, her voice filled with anticipation.

David rubbed the bridge of his nose, a sense of foreboding washing over him. "Well, I'm here now..." "Come here! I want to give you your present now!" she exclaimed, grabbing his hand and pulling him towards the sound of her voice. He reluctantly followed, wondering what she had in store for him. He stood at the doorway of her bedroom, his apprehension growing with each step. "Sit down and close your eyes!" she exclaimed, her voice bubbling with excitement. David hesitated for a moment, then cautiously sat on the edge of the bed and closed his eyes, bracing himself for whatever surprise she had planned.

As he sat there, he could hear the rustling of fabric and the crinkling of plastic, sounds that did little to ease his growing anxiety. "Jennifer, what are you..." She hushed him with her finger. "You promised you wouldn't say anything!" He sighed, realizing he had no choice but to play along. "Okay, I won't."

As he sat on the bed, he felt his pants unfasten and the sensation of heavy breathing close to him. He felt his pants being shuffled down his legs, a wave of heat rising within him. "Can I open my eyes now?" he asked, his voice slightly strained. "No, not yet!" she replied, her voice breathy and excited.

Although he couldn't see, he could feel and hear her movements. She grabbed his cock with her hand, her touch both gentle and firm. She started sucking it from base to tip several times until it stood completely erect, throbbing with anticipation. The sound of a package crinkling broke the silence, followed by a cool feeling on the tip of his penis as she sheathed a condom over his erection. David recalled the small bag she had carried out of the store yesterday and a smile crept across his face. He had a feeling he knew what was coming next. "Open your eyes," she whispered, her voice playful and inviting.

David slowly opened his eyes and was captivated by the sight before him. A petite blonde girl, completely naked, stood before him, her eyes sparkling with a mixture of nervousness and desire. The only thing she wore was a dog collar around her neck, a provocative touch that sent a shiver down his spine. She climbed into his lap and slowly lowered herself down onto him, her movements deliberate and sensual. Once settled, she took a moment to catch her breath, her chest rising and falling rapidly. While she was still, he took a moment to examine the collar she wore, the cool metal a stark contrast to her warm skin. "This was my present?" he asked, his voice deep and amused.

She nodded her head, her eyes locked on his, and bit down on her bottom lip, a silent invitation to lose himself in her. She started slowly, her movements hesitant at first, but nothing about this girl was gentle or soft. She bucked, she grinded, she clawed. She tried to fuck him with everything she had, but after her sixth orgasm, she had no strength left.

Deciding to turn her desire against her, he picked her up like a crew-served weapon and positioned her in an efficiently fuckable pose, before unleashing hell inside of her. After more than forty-five minutes, her entire body was shaking. Red marks covered nearly every part of her body he could reach, and her hair was a tangled mess.

David had used both condoms, but she lost nearly two pounds in water weight. He fetched her a cup of water and washed up in the bathroom before returning. "Happy Birthday master," she mumbled, exhausted but content. David leaned down and kissed her head before cleaning up, a satisfied smile playing on his lips. The present he had received was certainly one he wouldn't forget anytime soon.

The next day at school, David was sitting in his government class, trying to concentrate on the lecture, when he felt a poke in his ribs. He sighed, knowing who it was without even turning around. "What is it, Summer?" he asked, his voice laced with a hint of exasperation. "Did you go see Jennifer yesterday?" she asked, her tone casual but her eyes sharp. He sighed again. "Yes, I did." "How is she doing?" Summer pressed, her gaze unwavering.

David smiled, remembering the previous day's events. "She's taking another day off. We should go see her tomorrow." Summer sat back in her chair, her expression unreadable. "That's funny. She sounded fine to me when I spoke to her on the phone last night." He smiled to himself, amused by her jealousy and the secret they shared, as he continued his work, the memory of Jennifer's birthday present still fresh in his mind.

Chapter 11

Not According to Plan

That following weekend, David was at home when he heard knocking at his door. He went to answer the door, and Summer was standing on the porch. "Good morning, Summer, come on in." He swung the door open as he turned back inside, returning to the kitchen to finish making coffee. Summer sat on the couch, waiting for him to finish. David brought his coffee with him and sat down. Summer was studying his face and noticed that he wasn't in the best mood.

"What's the matter? You seem off today," she asked. David took a sip of his coffee, staring off as if lost in thought. "I think I fucked up, and I don't know if I can fix it." Summer was shocked, David was usually very methodical and for him to admit such a thing had to be serious. "Is this something recent, or does it have to do with your dream?" she asked. He paused, "The latter." She grabbed his coffee with one hand and his hand with the other, leading him to his room.

After they sat down, Summer started, "Let's keep that conversation in here." David pulled out one of his notebooks and put it on the desk. "Why don't you tell me what you were trying to do first." He took a deep breath. "I had three sons from my marriage, and they were my greatest joy, but their mother and I divorced after more than fifteen years. A few months after everything happened, they were killed by scavengers, and I've been trying to get them back." Summer stared, dumbfounded. "You had three sons?" He nodded. "Were you trying to have the same three children?" "Yes," he said as he lowered his head. Summer reached out to hug him, stroking her fingers through his hair as she held his head close to her chest. "I think what you're asking for is impossible, but why don't you tell me how you messed up."

Summer listened while David explained the complicated series of events that led him to marry his wife, which subsequently gave him his children. She took a long breath, "So let me get this straight; Your evil ex-girlfriend Donna ruined your life, followed you to your new job and you two broke up. She became friends with your mutual co-worker Sarah, that you hit it off with and then later they both got arrested for burglary because Donna's friend had a stick up his ass?" he nodded. "So, because you were with Sarah at the time, you became friends with her parents, then Sarah had to move back in with her ex-boyfriend because she had to pay legal fines after being arrested?" "Yup, that sounds right." "Then Sarah's parents introduced you to your future ex-wife?" He nodded, "That pretty much sums it up." "What the fuck was wrong with you?!" she exclaimed while punching him in the chest.

"Stop hitting me!" he whined. "So, because you never gave Donna a chance, everything else just fell apart?"

she asked. "Yes, that's a simple way of putting it," he replied. Summer grabbed his hand, "Look, even if you did create the exact same circumstances that led you to her, there's still no guarantee you would get those children, and even if you did, how would you really feel about them, how would they feel about the circumstances of their conception?" David shook his head, "I know you're right, but I at least wanted to try, I just didn't realize how impossible it was." Summer moved closer, "You know, just because you can't have the same children, doesn't mean you can't have other children." She whispered quietly in his ear.

David reached out, grabbing her neck with one hand. Her look was one of shock, but immediately melted into a smile, just before he leaned his face close to hers. Before her lips even touched his, she formed a hook with her tongue, immediately going all in. Rather than making out like a couple high schoolers hiding from their parents, she immediately pulled his hand and stuffed it under her shirt, holding his hand on her breast as she attempted to tongue polish the inside of his mouth. David had always thought she was shy, so nearly everything she did surprised him.

He laid her back on the bed, sliding his hands down her pants, as she reached down with both hands to grab his now erect cock. As his fingers slid against her labia, he could already feel how wet she was, gently spreading it all around the opening near her clit. She gripped him tightly as he gently rubbed his wet fingers along her inner labia until his middle finger slid inside of her. In only a few seconds, her movements stopped, her jaw seemed to lock open, and she began to whine as she came right onto his fingers and into his hand. David smiled, "You are a very sensitive girl." She couldn't speak, but her eyebrows furrowed as her orgasm began to fade.

David sat up and put his fingers in his mouth. She immediately winced at the sight, "Stop that, you're gross!" He smiled. As he got up to wash his hands, Summer looked around his room, her eyes drawn to the red envelope on the bookshelf. She picked up the envelope and a piece of paper slid out and fluttered to the ground. As she picked it up, he appeared at the door. "Being nosy?" She fumbled as she put the card and the piece of paper back on the shelf.

David picked up the piece of paper and handed it to Summer. "I bought another prom ticket." She looked at the ticket, then back at David, "How many people are going with you to prom?" He looked at the ticket, then back at her, "If you're included, that makes three. She tried to pout, but it came out as a laugh. "How are you going to escort three girls to prom?" He thought for a minute, "Well, Tiffany never went to her senior prom either and this was her gift for my birthday. Summer thought for a moment, "Prom is at the end of the year, when is your birthday?" "Next week, on Tuesday," he replied.

She sat down on his bed, hands in her lap, "What are you going to do, now that your plans to bring your kids back fell through?" As he flopped in his chair, he took a deep breath, "I don't know yet. I still have to prepare for what's coming." Summer thought for a moment, "Why don't we work as a team, you know, deal with this together?" David opened his book and flipped through the pages, "No, there is no team. It has to be my way, or it can't happen at all." She crawled into his lap, "Then tell us what we're supposed to do."

David spent his birthday at work, so nobody could celebrate on his behalf. His coworker Sarah broke up with her boyfriend, as he had expected, but he never participated in her housewarming party the following week. At home, he was reviewing his budget and while recording his earnings, he logged his current savings in his notebook. $9500 in two years. With new expenses and the up-and-coming prom, he had spent more money than he expected but was still able to save more than he ever had in the past.

Two months before prom, David was in class writing in his notebook when he felt a poke against his ribcage. David turned quickly, "Summer, you have really got to stop poking me!" She smiled, showing no concern on her face, "Come eat lunch with me today." David turned away before responding, "Sure, I'll go with you to lunch." After class, he met Summer just outside of the career center, on the way to his locker, she walked rigidly, gripping her books tightly in both arms. Conversely, David leisurely held his books in one hand, as his other arm hung freely while he walked.

Jennifer was waiting by his locker as he arrived with Summer in tow. As he put his books in his locker, the girls were engaged in excited conversation. Summer's posture was shy and composed, but she spoke with a hint of authority. She wore a loose button-up white shirt, tucked into fitted light blue jeans, white socks and flat shoes. Jennifer had a more playful and immature posture and wore a wide-neck black t-shirt, a pleated maroon skirt that ended just above the knees, tall black socks and black combat boots with heels, not to mention the black choker.

After he closed his locker, the three of them walked toward the cafeteria. Envious glances surrounded him as they passed through the crowded hallway, causing Jennifer to smile. The three sat in the hallway, just beyond the band hall at the top of a set of steps. Summer took a sandwich out of her bag and as she held it, she said, "Has David ever told you about Tiffany?" Jennifer wasn't paying attention. "What?" Summer repeated, "Has David ever mentioned Tiffany to you?" Jennifer paused for a moment before responding, "He doesn't really talk about other people, but I've heard my friends talking about her. Why, what's going on?"

David watched the conversation unfold, uncertainty creeping into his mind. Summer took a bite of her sandwich before continuing, "Apparently her birthday present is that she's going to be his date for the prom." Jennifer looked at David before turning back to Summer. "Is she old enough to buy alcohol?" she asked with a serious tone. David immediately reached out and slapped her on the thigh, causing her to jump. "Ouch! That hurt!"

David looked scornfully at Jennifer before turning to Summer, "I didn't come here to be thrown under the bus, if you wanted to conspire against me, you could have waited until I left." Summer smiled, taking another bite of her sandwich. Jennifer sat on the step below him but never took out her lunch. "Jennifer, did you bring a lunch today?" he asked. She shook her head, refusing to make eye contact. David reached into his wallet and pulled out a $5 bill, rubbing it on the back of her neck, "Go and get something to eat, and don't forget your lunch next time." Jennifer jumped to her feet and ran back up the hallway.

Summer lowered her hands into her lap, holding onto what was left of her sandwich. "Do you think it would be wise to talk to her about your plans?" He shook his head, "No, that's not something I want to burden her with just yet." Summer groaned in acceptance as she finished her lunch. David leaned his back against the wall, facing Summer, "What did you think of Jennifer's question?" he asked. "About buying alcohol?" she replied with a bite still in her mouth. David nodded. "I don't want to drink, if that's okay." He shrugged and looked away. She stared at him a moment before asking, "Do you drink?" He shook his head, "Not really, though I'm not against it per-se."

Jennifer returned with a Snapple and a bowl of nachos, hiding her food from David's disappointing gaze. As she sat down, he chuckled, shaking his head. "Jennifer, what are your plans for prom?" Summer asked. Jennifer was swallowing her bite as she prepared to answer. "My mother wants me home right after, so there isn't much I can do." Summer smiled. "Why, why do you ask?" she replied curiously. "Summer prepared to take a drink as she answered, "Because I want to have sex." David coughed and Jennifer nearly choked on her food. "Who are you trying to have sex with?" Jennifer asked frantically. Summer smiled as she took a drink of her water.

Jennifer's eyes lit up with intrigue as her eyes shifted between David and Summer. "You two haven't had sex yet?" Summer spit out her drink and David looked at Jennifer, shocked at her audacity. Summer wiped her mouth before replying, "No, no, of course not." Jennifer's eyes lowered as Summer looked at her curiously, "Have you?" she asked. Jennifer blushed as she lowered her head. Summer's shocked gaze shot between her and David. Her heart began to race as her curiosity built up, "What was it like?" leaning toward her. Jennifer waved her finger with food in her mouth. As she struggled to swallow, she finally answered, "I felt like I was going to die!" David rolled his eyes at her response.

A look of terror fell on Summer's face hearing this news. Seeing this, Jennifer waved her hands frantically, "It wasn't bad, in fact, it was great, I just wasn't prepared for it as much as I thought I was." Summer calmed down a little, looking at David. "I suppose a lifetime of experience comes with the territory," she said coquettishly. David rolled his eyes and looked away. The two girls finished their lunch and David stood, prepared to leave. He turned to Jennifer, "Jennifer, I'm going to start teaching you how to drive a stick starting next weekend." Then turning to Summer, "So we can either keep tutoring on Sunday morning or move it to after school." Summer thought for a moment before responding, "After school is fine, just tell me which day."

The weekend arrived and Sunday morning David prepared to leave for his driving lessons. As he packed a lunch for the long afternoon, his mother approached, "Do you have any plans after school's out?" she asked. Without looking up, he responded, "Yes, I spoke to an Army recruiter last month and I'm going to be leaving for training in the fall." His mother lowered her eyes, "I see, what are you going to do?" David stopped, looking at his mother, "I'm going to be a cook, at least that's the plan." His mother nodded her head. "You know, if you were more diligent, you could have gone to college and became an officer, you're certainly smart enough." He blew off her comment before shouldering his pack. "I understand what you mean, but I know what I'm doing, so please don't worry about me."

David arrived at Jennifer's house just after early morning. He promptly walked to the door and knocked firmly on the wooden trim. Laura opened the door and let him in, wearing capri pants and a long t-shirt. As he sat waiting, Laura turned toward her daughter's bedroom,

"Hurry up Jennifer, your ride is here!" David sat in silence as the clamoring and crashing about could be heard from the living room. After several minutes, Jennifer emerged from the hallway, wearing a short, pleated skirt and a loose cardigan sweater. David examined her footwear and pointed at her feet, "You are going to want to change out of those boots, put on some sneakers or tennis shoes." Jennifer looked down, she had instinctively donned her high heeled boots." After several more minutes, she emerged wearing a pair of converse style shoes.

The two left the house and Jennifer waited by the driver's door, David gestured toward the passenger door and said, "You aren't driving on the road yet." She responded in affirmation before walking around to the other side of the car. David drove to the Activity Center on the north side of town, a popular location for teaching new drivers. David parked the car and the two switched seats. "Before you can drive, you need to understand the relationship between the clutch, the transmission, and the engine, as well as how the shift knob is used." Jennifer nodded her head as she played with the shifter.

With nearly an hour of detailed exposition, Jennifer felt she was ready to start driving. The first two hours were a series of failed launches and stalled stops, for which she kept apologizing, but David constantly reassured her. By midafternoon, she was driving freely through the parking lot, making no attempt to adhere to the markings on the asphalt, though she never drove higher than second gear.

Her confidence was soaring as they drove aimlessly in circles, evident by her sudden desire to start a conversation. "When you leave after graduation, is there going to be any room for me?" she asked, feigning a confident disposition. David had not seriously considered her future up until this point, but considering recent revelations, had started to wonder what he might say to her if asked.

The two sat in the car, parked under a shade tree as they ate the lunch he had packed. It was late in the afternoon and their driving practice had come to an end. David said, "You have to finish school, and I have training, maybe by the time you finish, you will have thought about what you want to do, which may or may not include me." Jennifer smiled, "I want to make you proud, then you would want to keep me." He smiled as he finished his lunch. Early in the evening, he dropped her off, waving goodbye to her mother as she stared out the window.

The following afternoon after school, Summer arrived at his door, still wearing her clothes from school. David thought for a moment after opening the door. "Is there some kind of unspoken uniform for high school girls?" She was confused, "No, what are you talking about?" He let her in, walking to his room. "I just noticed that your outfit seems to be a staple for female upperclassmen." It hadn't dawned on her at the time, but his observation seemed to be on point. She sat down, untucking her shirt, "Was it always like this?" she asked.

"Yes, I thought maybe it was a fad or something, but you seem to be unaware of it."

The two sat in a long silence for several minutes as Summer fidgeted with her fingers on his bed. "What's on your mind?" he asked, concerned. She shook her head, "I was just thinking, but it's not important." David leaned forward, whispering, "Are you horny?" Her eyes grew wide at his question, "Eww, no! Why would you ask me that?" he chuckled as he sat back, "Well I'm no clairvoyant and you brought it up the other day."

Her outburst quieted and she went back to fidgeting, "What if we got married?" Her heart pounding in her chest as she waited for his response. David's posture and expression didn't change, putting her on edge. "I actually considered that, but I didn't want to bring it up." Her eyes grew wide at his response, as she looked up at him.

"What were you thinking?" she asked expectantly. David looked down at his notebook briefly before responding, "Obviously my plans have changed and there's no denying the financial and social benefits of being married, so I figured, If I were married, I could still retain the same benefits as before, keeping my path in line with my goals." Summer frowned at his response, "So this would be a business marriage?" David nodded his head, "Yes, but there are always fringe benefits to every business relationship." Her smile gradually returned, revealing some hidden intention. "What happens when the arrangement has satisfied its purpose?" David responded without hesitation, "Then we get divorced, plain and simple." Summer nodded her head, she secretly hoped that by marrying him, she would eventually win him over completely, but her understanding told her otherwise.

David had no reservations taking three women to prom, so it was safe to assume that he would carry on in the same manner once he became an independent adult. Just as long as she served his purposes and didn't disrupt his plans, he would keep her as long as she was willing to comply. At least in this way, they could be a team, and she would have a strong ally on her side.

Nearly two months had passed and the three sat in an empty classroom eating lunch. Jennifer had satisfied her driving requirements for her license, except for the completion of her driver's education course. While Summer had started her own notebook, making plans of her own, inspired by David's meticulous attention to detail. Prom was the following day, and all students were going to be released at noon, allowing time for the faculty and staff to prepare for the event.

"What's the plan for tomorrow?" Jennifer asked, looking at David. "I haven't heard back from Tiffany, but if she shows up, I'll take her to pick up Summer, then you. Just make sure you're ready by 5:00pm." Everyone appeared calm, but their collective heartbeat could be felt through the tabletop. "Would it be okay with you if we all stayed together after school?" Summer suggested. David thought for a moment before responding, "Sure, but we're going to have to go by everyone's house either way." Jennifer interjected, still chewing on her food, "But if we bring our dresses with us in the morning, we won't have to." David slapped his hands down onto the table, letting out a deep sigh. "Fine, if that's what you want, who am I to argue!" The girls shared knowing glances before continuing their lunch.

Chapter 12

A Breach of Trust

It was finally Friday, and graduation was a week away, however, tonight was going to be a big night. As he put his books in his locker, Jennifer and Summer waited behind him, impatiently. "Let's go," he said, waving his arms forward as if herding children. The three walked toward the parking lot, standing on either side of David as they struggled to keep up with his gape. David had picked Summer up from her house first, then Jennifer, nearly causing all three of them to be late for school. They each carried hangers, draped in plastic over their respective dresses for that evening. David didn't bother bringing his tuxedo, as he would be going home immediately after school.

David parked his car in the driveway, as Jennifer looked around. "This is where you live?" He hadn't thought about it before, but Jennifer had never been to his house. Summer lived in the same neighborhood, but her house was several blocks to the northwest along a shared road. As they retrieved their dresses from the trunk of his car, he unlocked the front door and went inside, leaving the door wide open. Summer casually walked to his room and hung her dress up in the closet, followed by a suspicious Jennifer. "How many times has she been to your house?" she asked.

David didn't answer but immediately went to the refrigerator to get a drink. Jennifer put her dress next to Summer's and sat on the chair, as Summer waited on the bed.

David went outside the back door and took out a pack of cigarettes, lighting one as he stood on the back porch. Several minutes later, Jennifer followed him out, not saying a word. After a minute, Summer followed, surprised at the sight. "David, when did you start smoking?" she gasped. Jennifer sat on a chair, not saying a word as David answered, "When I was 14." She thought for a moment before asking, "The whole time?" He nodded, "I had quit several times, but with little else available, I eventually came back to it." She didn't want to argue but was still surprised at how she was unable to detect it for the past few years. David snuffed his cigarette before continuing, "It's my bad habit, not yours, so you shouldn't have to bear the burden of it."

The three went back into the house and David went to his room. "We still have several hours before we need to start getting ready, so what would you like to do?" Neither of the two girls had considered this when they talked the day before. "Where are your parents?" Jennifer asked. "They're both at work and my brother won't be home for a few hours." Summer stood up, "Well, in that case, I'm going to walk home and grab my makeup kit." David nodded. "Would you like to come with me?" she asked

Jennifer. "No, but can I use some of your makeup when you get back?" Summer nodded, "Sure, no problem."

As Summer left, Jennifer immediately jumped on David's lap, wasting no time in taking advantage of the opportunity. He didn't have to ask her intentions, and had no desire to stop her, so he let her continue. She began by kissing and sucking on his neck and shoulders, as if his skin was made of hardened candy. Settling on his lips, she kissed him deeply as she grinded her body into him, bucking her hips as he held onto her waist. She promptly stood up, removing her bike shorts from under her skirt, followed by her shirt. David watched as she removed key articles of clothing, not bothering to do the same. When she finished, she unbuckled his belt, focused like it was a timed practical exercise. With his pants now down around his ankles, she straddled, then lowered herself onto him, hugging him tightly as he filled her up.

Meanwhile, Summer was carrying her makeup kit in hand, a modest assortment of blushes, eyeliner and lip gloss in a small zipper pouch, as she arrived back at David's house. She opened the door and walked toward his room when the sounds of moaning stopped her just outside the door. She stood outside his bedroom door, frozen at the realization of what was happening just on the other side. While she considered interrupting the two, she began to hear Jennifer's voice through the door, "Please keep fucking me master, oh God yes! I am a little bitch; I like being my master's bitch!" Summer gasped as she covered her mouth with her hand. She had never imagined they would do it at a time like this. Then it hit her, why should she hide, it's not like she was in the wrong, after all, if they got caught, it's their own fault.

She pushed the door open slowly and quietly stepped inside. The chair was facing the bed, which left Jennifer's back to the door, however, David clearly saw Summer entering the room, but didn't say a word. She set the makeup kit down and sat on the edge of the bed, waiting for Jennifer to finish. David and Summer began to have a silent dialogue using hand gestures while Jennifer was distracted with her own actions. Summer shrugged her shoulders, shaking her head. David pointed toward Summer's makeup bag then the door and finally at Jennifer, Summer nodded. "Fuck! God damnit!" Jennifer shrilled as she began to shake. Summer then pointed to her wrist with one finger, tapping it twice, then pointing down at her feet. David made a thinking gesture with his thumb and forefinger before holding up six fingers. Summer raised her eyebrows and nodded her head.

As Jennifer sat limp in David's lap, Summer cleared her throat, causing Jennifer to jump and David to start laughing. "How long have you been here?" Jennifer asked, while rushing to put her shirt on. Summer smiled, "Only a few minutes." Jennifer grabbed her shorts and sat on the edge of the bed, blushing and embarrassed. David broke the awkward silence, "Did you get everything you needed?" Summer lifted her makeup kit, "Yep, got it here."

"Good," he responded. "Jennifer, it might be a good idea for you to take a shower first, then Summer, then I'll go. You two can get ready and I'll make lunch." Jennifer nodded without saying a word, still embarrassed. "I have a few shirts and shorts for you to wear, so you don't have to put on your dresses yet," he mentioned.

Jennifer grabbed the clothes and ran to the bathroom as David leaned over to pull his pants back up. Before reaching his knees, Summer stopped him, putting her hands on his. David looked up, confused, "What is it?" Summer didn't respond, but began to kneel down, biting her lip. David was slightly embarrassed, but didn't say anything further. As he sat back, resigning to the situation, she reached down, examining him thoroughly. "It smells funny," she said as she held it close to her face. "That would probably be Jennifer," he responded. "Oh, I see." She didn't dwell on the obvious and started running her tongue along its base. "It's getting warmer," she exclaimed with joyful curiosity. David was still sensitive, and the situation was already more than he had bargained for.

Summer stood up and unbuttoned her pants, revealing her plain white cotton panties that hugged her hips firmly. She wasn't as curvy as Jennifer, and her hips weren't as wide, but he didn't mind. David reached out and slid her panties down, revealing her neatly tucked lips. She stumbled as he pulled her forward, sliding his body lower in his chair. She lifted the hem of her shirt up as he began to lick her from bottom to top, causing her knees to buckle under her weight. As she struggled to remain standing, he held her hips firmly to his face as he dug into her, using his tongue. He pushed his tongue deep, as if scooping ice cream from the bottom of a cone just as she began to clench her body. Just then, a warm, sweet and slightly sticky fluid began to run down his chin and her hips began to shake, throwing her off balance.

Summer collapsed to the ground, sitting on her legs as she tried to catch her breath. David stood and picked her up, setting her on the bed. "I have to make lunch," he said, as he ran his fingers through her hair. In the kitchen sink, he washed his hands and rinsed his face before taking out the ingredients to make a full meal. Jennifer came out of the bathroom, wearing a comically oversized t-shirt and shorts that barely contained her ass. "What are you making?" she asked. "Rice and chicken," he responded. As he answered, he could see Summer sneaking to the bathroom, still wearing only her shirt. He smiled before turning his attention back to his cooking.

After finishing lunch, he placed the food on the table with a couple plates and flatware. As everyone ate, Summer and Jennifer smiled at each other, as David watched. "What are you two smiling about?" he asked. Summer shook her head, "Nothing." Jennifer, with a mouth half full of food said, "It feels really domestic having lunch together!" Immediately, David understood why they were smiling. "Well, don't take too long, we have to start getting ready in a couple of hours." The girls nodded without looking up from their meals.

David took a shower next, leaving the others at the table to discuss whatever it is that girls talk about. After about fifteen minutes, he emerged from the shower, wrapped in a towel and walked into his room. There, both girls were sitting on his bed, still wearing his shirts and shorts. "Have you two finished?" "Yes, we even rinsed off the dishes," Jennifer said proudly. "It was my idea," Summer added, eliciting a scowl from Jennifer. David started to get dressed, showing no consideration for the others in his room. "When is Tiffany supposed to be here?" Jennifer asked. "I don't know," he responded while putting on lotion.

It was nearly 3:00pm when he heard a knock at his door. "Could you get that?" David asked, not quite dressed. Summer stood up and left the room. As David was putting on his shirt, Summer stood in the doorway to his bedroom. "You have company," she said nervously. David raised his head to see a tall blonde, hair down to the middle of her back, carrying a garment bag. "Tiffany! I'm surprised you managed to get here so soon," he said enthusiastically. Tiffany looked around the room at the other two people and asked, "Which one is Jennifer?" Jennifer raised her hand. Pointing to Summer, she asked, "Then who is this?" David stood straight before answering, "This is Summer, my classmate." Tiffany squinted her eyes, examining everyone's state of dress. After a brief moment to take in her surroundings, she let out a deep breath, "I guess we're all going together?" David stopped while passing her in the doorway, "Yes," kissing her on the cheek.

Tiffany took charge of helping the others get ready as David put on his tuxedo. She was the only one that brought a curling iron, so the others took turns having their hair done up, while David waited in the living room. Just after 3:30 his younger brother came home, followed by his mother. "David, you look so nice in your tuxedo. Is your date here? I saw the other car," his mother asked. "Yes, their getting ready now," he responded. Summer was the first to come out of the bedroom, wearing a long strapless silver dress, a black choker and sterling earrings. His mother gasped at the sight, rushing over to look her over as she doted on her shamelessly. David rolled his eyes at his mother. "Stop embarrassing her," he said in a mildly frustrated voice. "I have to take a picture!" she said excitedly as she rushed to her room to get her camera.

After she took a picture of the two standing together, she looked at David while charging the film, "Is there still somebody in there?" gesturing to the bedroom. David sat back down, smiling, as Summer sat next to him on the couch. The bedroom door opened and out stepped a petite short haired blonde, wearing a long dark blue dress with arm cuffs and a black choker. David's mother looked at the new arrival with confusion, "Where's her date? Are they sisters?" David shook his head, "No, and I'm her date." His mother was confused, looking at both girls for some kind of answer, but none was given. Just as she gained her composure, she gestured for Jennifer to stand up for another picture. Right when she was about to take another picture, David's bedroom door opened again, this time revealing a mature, long-haired blonde with a flowing red dress, gold earrings and a lace choker.

David's mother let out a deep sigh, "What the hell is going on here, are you their chauffeur?" she said in an exasperated tone. "No mother, they're with me." As they all filed out of the door, David's mother hung her head. Seconds after the door shut, it opened suddenly. She looked up to see her husband enter the house. "Was that Tiffany I saw just now?" he asked, pointing outside. His mother collapsed on the couch, sighing deeply, "Probably, but I hope that wasn't the first thing you noticed."

As David pulled up to the valet in front of the activity center, teachers dressed the part took his keys as three blonde women wearing long dresses and chokers stepped out of his car, causing a cascade of turning heads to follow their entrance as all four climbed the stairs. David walked up front with Tiffany on his right, Jennifer on his left and Summer on Jennifer's left. After casually greeting some of their classmates, David and Summer danced first, as Tiffany and Jennifer explored the buffet, after all, it was their class. After returning to their table, two drinks were waiting for them as they arrived, along with the two other girls, chatting in the dimly lit ballroom.

David took turns with each girl, and at times was with two or all three throughout the night. At one point in the night, all four were seated at the table and Summer brought up the topic they were all wondering at some point during the evening. "David, how many girls have you been with?" This question immediately captured the attention of the other two as David thought about how to answer the question. David took a drink as he responded, "You mean in the biblical sense?" Jennifer laughed as Tiffany nearly spit out her drink. "Do you count?" he asked, pointing to Summer, who then shook her head. With the same hand holding his drink, he extended two fingers. Tiffany and Jennifer both blushed, before Summer interjected, "What about before?" David narrowed his eyes, he knew what she was trying to do, but didn't have the heart to scold her in front of the others. "I think ten, he said seriously." The room seemed to go silent as the four of them leaned in, as if to shield their conversation from the world.

David reluctantly began to list his partners chronologically, giving each of them nicknames, the evil ex-girlfriend, the coworker, the ex-wife, the former student, the horse trainer, the disgruntled wife, the massage therapist, and the bank teller. Tiffany and Jennifer were shocked, dread washing over their faces as Summer continued asking questions. "Which one was the girlfriend you mentioned?" David shook his head, "She's not on that list." Tiffany's expression suddenly changed, then asked, "What the hell are you two talking about, what girlfriend?"

Summer briefly explained David's dream to the others as he said nothing. The conversation continued for several more minutes until the music finally quieted down, as the band took a short break.

David watched the other's faces, trying to gauge their thoughts based on their expressions. Summer was calm, a determined look on her face as she looked at the others. Tiffany was lost in thought, as if trying to work it all out in her head. Meanwhile, Jennifer just smiled, happy to be invited. As Summer stood to go to the bathroom, Jennifer followed, and Tiffany moved closer to David, a determined look in her eyes. "Does that mean I don't have to wait for you anymore?" David nearly fell out of his chair at her question. "After all of that, that's what you were wondering about?" he asked, shock in his voice. She shrugged, "I don't know, it all seems kind of far-fetched, but if coming back forty years was actually possible, then everything else about you makes perfect sense, so why not?" David was surprised at her reasoning. "I think I should reward you for your loyalty," he said as he kissed her hand.

When the girls returned, they all decided to have their pictures taken. First as couples, then all of them together. After nearly three hours into the night, David gathered all the girls together and announced their departure. Tiffany made a pout face and asked, "Why do we have to leave so soon? It doesn't end until 10:00pm." Jennifer raised her hand, "My mother said I have to be home at 9:00." As everyone gathered their things, the four left the center, happy that they were able to avoid the rush. David had Jennifer sit in the front seat this time, while Summer sat in the back seat on the passenger side.

As David stopped in front of Jennifer's house, he could see her mother looking out the window, relieved he kept her curfew. David walked her to the door and before going inside, she kissed him once on the lips, cuing a choir of cheers from the car. After Jennifer went inside her house, David returned to the car, this time, Tiffany had taken the front seat. David looked in his rear-view mirror at Summer. "Am I taking you home next? Sitting back and crossing her arms, she shook her head, "Nope, I'm not going." David didn't argue, but as he started driving, he looked back and said, "Unless you want me to drop you off somewhere else, you're going home, because you can't stay at my house." Tiffany grabbed the top of his hand, leaning back in her seat and said casually, "I told her she can stay with me tonight."

David didn't question her decision, but asked, "You aren't going home tonight?" She shook her head, "No, I was expecting to stay out later than this, so I rented a room." David's brain began to tingle at her words, understanding the implications of her statement. "Was this your plan the whole time?" he asked. She nodded her head, smiling as she turned her gaze back to the road. David followed her directions and the three of them arrived at the Fairfield Inn.

As the three of them entered the main entrance, David could only imagine the thoughts of the hotel staff and other guests watching them as they filed into the elevator. The three rode up to the third floor without saying a word. Finally arriving at her room, Tiffany opened the door, and they entered, one after the other. David examined the room; it was a small room with two queen-sized beds and a small sofa. "Tiffany, how many people were you expecting here?" he asked. Tiffany was in the bathroom removing her earrings and cleaning off her makeup when she responded, "Just Sandra and me, but she's staying at her parents' tonight." Summer fell back on one of the beds and kicked off her shoes. "I'm going to go downstairs and get your clothes from the back of the car," he said as he grabbed the card key off the counter.

Chapter 13

Changing the Past

David arrived at his car, but didn't grab the clothes from the trunk. He sat on the hood, watching traffic pass on the highway next to him as he pulled a cigarette from its pack. "Are you hiding from me?" He jumped at the sudden question. Tiffany had followed him downstairs, wearing shorts and a t-shirt. "No, I just wasn't prepared to deal with Summer's bullshit tonight," he said, passing a cigarette to her. As she sat next to him, she leaned her head on his shoulder. "Just because you've got more experience, doesn't mean you have all the answers. I think she genuinely wants to help, and you don't like giving up control." He chuckled. "What's so funny?" she asked. David shook his head, "Nothing, it's just that, I've been told that before." Tiffany smiled. "Did one of your hoes tell you that?" she teased. "No, my girlfriend." Tiffany's smile became serious, "Are you going to save her too?" He nodded his head, "If I can."

After putting out his cigarette, David grabbed Tiffany's bag and Summer's clothes out of the trunk, then he and Tiffany went back upstairs. Summer was still on the bed, arms and legs sprawled out in four directions. As he set the clothes down, Tiffany leaned close to his ear, "I'm going to take a shower, don't be too hard on her." She kissed him before retreating into the bathroom. Summer sat up, propping her body up onto her elbows. David looked back at Summer, "You seem to have a hard time knowing when to keep your mouth shut," he said, as he approached the foot of the bed.

Summer didn't respond, but her expression conveyed a feeling of apprehension and excitement. He reached for Tiffany's bag, removing the shoulder strap. "Put your wrists together," he commanded. With her wrists together, he made a simple cuff knot around her wrists using the strap, before securing it to the corner of the bed. With his tie, he secured her left ankle, tying it to the opposite corner. With one swift move, he grabbed her right leg, flipping her over onto her stomach, like a lamb on a spit, her dress twisting around her legs. Reaching up, he pulled her undergarments down past her feet, leaving them near the corner where his tie bound her ankle. After unzipping her back, he lifted the bottom of her dress, pulling it over her head, exposing her pale naked skin.

Summer's free leg bent as she tried to flip her body onto her back. Suddenly a loud slap stopped her movement. David had slapped her hard on the ass, pushing her leg back down as she jerked from the impact. Positioning himself between her legs, he leaned on the back of her knee, completely immobilizing her. Summer's head was completely covered by her dress, so she couldn't see what he was about to do, but every time she said anything, he slapped her ass hard enough to leave a bright handprint.

Tiffany had come out of the shower, and David gestured for her to be quiet, pointing to the other bed, closest to her. Tiffany sat quietly, not making a sound.

Using Tiffany's belt, he flogged Summer's butt, back and thighs until her entire back side was pink, leaving only her shoulders, arms and calves untouched. Summer began to whimper, the sound muffled by her own dress. When he was satisfied, he flipped her back over, exposing her untouched front end. Summer didn't move, breathing heavily as she struggled to keep her composure. David stood as Tiffany watched from the other bed, a look of terror and curiosity on her face. On her back, he continued the onslaught, occasionally pinching her nipples until she yelped, recoiling from the pain.

At this point, David had lost the appetite for cruelty and untied her. He pulled her dress back down and sat at the foot of the bed. Summer recoiled to the head of the bed, hugging her legs as tears ran down her cheeks. The three sat in complete silence for several minutes until David began to speak. In his monologue, he described the last 13 years of his former life, how he was cast out of his home, because he wasn't trusted to lead his family. He talked about his children and their families, how they were found slaughtered in their homes, completely unprepared for life's hardships. He talked about how he waited nearly a decade to meet his true love, only to see her for the first time, decomposing in a bathtub, swarming with flies and larva.

Summer and Tiffany listened as he described the cruelties he faced; the people he watched die and even the people he killed. His kindness and sacrifice had caused him more pain and loss than any one person could endure, and he regret not being able to save anyone, even the woman on the bus was lost before he met her. As he spoke, his voice became raw, his emotions burdened by years of death and destruction. Summer wept bitterly, her legs unfolding as she began to crawl toward him. David closed his eyes when he finished talking, hanging his head as Summer pulled his face to hers. Her tear-covered face pressed up against his as she kissed him desperately, falling into his lap as he fell back from the weight.

Still wearing her dress, Summer straddled him, covering his entire lower body in silver fabric. As she kissed him, she pulled off his shirt, repeatedly getting caught on his arms and neck as each piece was discarded onto the floor. David sat up, moving to the head of the bed with Summer still hanging onto him. With the bodice already falling loose, she pushed it down before pressing her bare chest against his as she kissed him fiercely. David struggled to remove his pants under her as she dug her fingers into his neck. As his pants came free, she lifted her body up, giving him room to push them off. The feel of her skin brushing against his, tingled throughout his body as she moved her pelvis closer to his. She was thin, so there was less body than function, with less ass between his thin physique and hers, he could clearly tell she was already wet.

Out of the corner of his eye, he could see Tiffany on the other bed, wide eyed as she watched the two entangle themselves in a frenzy. David's lap was already soaking wet as Summer tried desperately to get him in, biting her lip and on the verge of cursing just before he felt her sliding down onto him. The initial penetration was met with no resistance, causing her to reflexively grip him tightly, as she grit her teeth. Tiffany gasped and Summer nearly screamed as her hymen was aggressively torn through. David held her tightly as she cried out, occasionally looking to Tiffany, who was trying not to be seen. After a few moments, Summer loosened her grip and began moving her body against his, pushing her hips down onto him as he held her close.

The entire time, she didn't let go, occasionally slowing down to let out a hyperventilating squeak as her body trembled under her dress. She collapsed in his arms after nearly half an hour, her limp body soaked in sweat as she tried to catch her breath. She had stopped crying, and her mascara dried to her cheeks. David held her for several minutes, occasionally looking at Tiffany who, at some point, decided to join in with her own solo act. Summer had passed out, so he rolled her to her side, removed her dress and covered her with the blanket. As he stood up, Tiffany quickly retracted her hands and looked innocently at David. "I should go take a shower," he said as he picked up the clothes around the bed.

As he walked to the bathroom, Tiffany followed him, but neither her nor David said anything as he washed himself off. Tiffany watched him with admiration the entire time. Since last year, he had grown several more inches and stood nearly four inches taller than her. He wasn't bulky, but his muscles were clearly defined, and her eyes couldn't help but wonder. David didn't bring a change of clothes, so he didn't bother looking for anything to wear after drying off. His shamelessness left Tiffany at a loss for words, leaving her writhing in her seat as she waited on him.

He crawled into the empty bed, joined by Tiffany, who wrapped her legs around him as he faced the middle of the room. Despite David's apparent reluctance, she was adamant, reaching around and grabbing him firmly. David's body made her feel like a toddler, his proximity filled her with an unrelenting desire to touch and put every part of him in her mouth. He turned around to face her, resting his hand on her ribs. She reached out, touching his face as her other hand rested on his chest, "David," she whispered. "Hmmm?" "I want to keep you," she said as she kissed him. David lifted off her shirt, rolling on top of her as she held onto his face.

He reached under her shoulders as she lifted her hands above her head, interlocking her fingers within his as he leveraged her body with every thrust. She didn't fight him once the entire time, allowing him to use her body, over and over again as she held onto him.

It was nearly midnight when they both fell asleep, with Tiffany holding onto his back as he faced the other bed. Shortly after 1:00am, Summer awoke, surprised at her state of undress. She searched frantically for David before spotting him in the other bed with Tiffany. Letting out a sigh of relief, Summer took a shower, only bothering to put on her shirt from the day before when she dried off. She casually crawled into bed and quickly went to sleep.

David woke up early, stretching his legs as he opened his eyes. The days of waking up with aching shoulders were long behind him, something he was not looking forward to in the future. As he looked around, he realized he was stuck in his sleeping position. Summer had crawled into the same bed and was curled up with her head tucked into his chest. Meanwhile, Tiffany was on the opposite side, sprawled out with her right leg hooked around his. David and Tiffany were completely naked and Summer wore an unbuttoned white shirt, with nothing else. As David lifted his head, he saw the time on the clock, it was 7:40am.

As he lowered his head, Summer's gaze surprised him. Unlike the blubbering mess from the night prior, her face was clean, and her eyes were clear, with a good night's sleep, she had recovered from the night before. Her smile was all it took for him to feel better about what he put her through the night prior. "How are you feeling?" he asked.

She blushed, looking down at his chest, "I'm okay, sorry if I seemed too excited yesterday." David was shocked, did she not remember what he did? Summer cuddled up to him, pushing her leg between his. Coincidently, Tiffany did the same. As their knees knocked together, both women sat up, looking over his shoulder at each other before making a silent agreement.

Again, Summer positioned her right leg between David's legs, as Tiffany wrapped her left leg over top of his, pulling herself tightly against his back. After several more minutes, all three decided that they needed to get up, hurrying to put on their clothes. The three didn't stay for the continental breakfast, considering their available attire. However, They did make plans to meet on Sunday morning, before Tiffany went back with Sandra.

David and the two girls left the hotel and got into the car. As they drove back to their neighborhood, Summer leaned the chair back and stared out the window. "Are your parents' going to be upset at you for coming home so late?" he asked. "No," shaking her head. "I told my dad that I was staying at a friend's house yesterday." For this reason, David decided to stop several houses away when he dropped her off. As he got ready to leave, Summer knocked on the window. "What is it?" he asked. "I'm coming over after lunch today," She said before turning around and walking toward her house.

David arrived at his house a little after 9:30am and Tiffany immediately got into her car to head back to the hotel. His mother, sitting in the living room. "How did it go last night?" she asked with one eyebrow raised. "It was a good night, but we had to leave early to take Jennifer home." His mother wasn't satisfied with his answer, but didn't persist. After taking a shower, he put on his casual clothes and sat at the table. David was legally an adult, so criticizing him seemed inappropriate, but his mother couldn't help herself. "Are you in a relationship with any of the three girls you had over yesterday?" He looked at his mother before smiling. "Technically, I do have some kind of relationship with all three, but none of them are my girlfriend." His mother sighed in relief.

For the next several hours, David cleaned and prepared lunch for his family. Secretly hoping that his contributions might spare his father's downfall, which would inevitably lead to his death. As he set the food on the table, someone knocked at the door. David was surprised Summer would arrive so early, not expecting her for another hour or so, but as he opened the door, Tiffany lunged at him, catching him off guard. David's parents looked at each other before looking at their guest. "Tiffany, it's nice to see you again," his father said, as if prompted by a cue card. Tiffany held onto David's arm, smiling as he guided her to the dining room.

"We were just about to eat lunch, but you can join us if you're hungry," his mother said. Tiffany didn't waste time and sat in the chair meant for David. His father grabbed food from the table and sat on the couch while his mother sat at the table, as if expecting an explanation from the couple. David's younger brother, after assessing the situation, retreated to his room with his food. His mother paused before asking, "What's the story with you two?" David looked at Tiffany, then she looked at his mother before answering, "I asked David to take me to prom, since I never went." His mother stared at David before asking her next question. "Have you two…" Knock-Knock-Knock! Interrupted by a knock at the door, everyone turned toward the noise, as his father got up to answer it.

After opening the door, his father looked toward the table, smiling, before turning around to sit back on the couch. Summer emerged from the doorway, sensing the tension in the atmosphere. "Hi, sorry if I'm interrupting," she said with a hint of amusement. Summer didn't hold back; she had been there several times and was already familiar with his family. His mother stared at Summer as she walked to the table, kissed David on the cheek and sat beside him. Before finishing her question, she stared at the door, as if expecting a third guest.

Summer and Tiffany didn't hide their flirtatious behavior, further aggravating his mother. "Which one of you is his girlfriend?" she asked, frustratingly. David continued eating his lunch, blissfully unconcerned at the drama he caused. Tiffany shook her head, looking at Summer, who also shook her head. "He's my friend," Tiffany answered. "He's my classmate," Summer added. His mother threw her hands in the air before leaving the table, stomping toward her room. The two only stayed for a few hours, because David had to work that night. When they left, Tiffany offered Summer a ride home and David started getting ready for work.

The next morning, David arrived at Jennifer's house at the normal time, this time, he let Jennifer drive the car on the road. Even though she still drove like a beginner, her handling of the clutch and stick were flawless. Jennifer picked Summer up from her house, while David rode in the passenger seat. Summer's posture and character had noticeably changed since the week prior. Before, she typically acted shy and self-conscious when alone, but now her disposition was relaxed and proud, especially around David.

The three met Tiffany at Denny's along the highway, a long-time favorite hangout of David's during his old high school years. There, they ordered food while only Tiffany and David ordered coffee. The four discussed their plans over breakfast. Tiffany was finishing her degree in Animal Science while Summer planned to join the Army Reserves as a medic while going to college to become a nurse practitioner. Jennifer had no concrete plans yet, but after meeting David, she leaned heavily on Hydroponic Agriculture, something he had some experience in from the past.

After breakfast, Tiffany gave Summer and Jennifer a hug before kissing David goodbye and the four went on their way. Summer was dropped off first, then Jennifer.

The next morning, School continued as usual, only most of the classes weren't handing out assignments. That following Friday, the Seniors had their high school graduation at the county seat's event center, only this time, David invited his parents along.

For David, his last summer at home started on a much higher note than he remembered. Sitting in his room, he started a new notebook, laying out his new plans for the years to come. Summer was going to start her Army training at the end of June, but David wasn't going to start his until the fall, so he sat with her for several days, brushing her up on what to expect while in training, even though he had no idea what to expect at her advanced individual training station, his military background far exceeded any training she would get as an initial entry trainee.

The last few weeks before Summer's departure, in addition to getting her up to speed on what to expect in the military, he had helped her apply for several colleges offering a nursing practitioner program, two of which worked with the local hospital. David was aware that the hospital would soon undergo a rapid expansion, so he urged her to pick one of these programs. In addition to helping her with her educational path, they would often sneak away, satisfying their primal urges in both intimate and shameless ways.

After Jennifer got her driver's license, David helped her find a part time job at a local greenhouse, only a quarter of a mile from her home. With her license in hand, they would allow her to drive the company truck, as long as she didn't take it to school or keep it longer than the next day. David had decided to help these girls cultivate their own future, knowing their loyalty to him, he was certain he could use their skills in his new plan.

As David waited for the summer to end, he thought about the past five years, reflecting on the changes he made in his own life. He stopped his bullying before it carried over into high school. He graduated at the top of his class, even though he never took college prep classes. He saved himself from a disastrous relationship which kept him from being arrested, expelled and costing him his enlistment bonus. He acquired several potential allies for his project. He cultivated his own strength and endurance, nearly doubling that of his former self, even as an adult. He managed to save more than $11,000 in 29 months. While he still mourned for his children and would miss the life he had with them, those memories would always be fresh in his mind as he started his life again, this time, with a more optimistic outlook.

Chapter 14

Domestic Experience

It was the fall after his eighteenth birthday and David was in processing at his Basic Combat Training reception unit when he saw all of the familiar faces. He made sure to pick the same departure date and occupation, so his training would remain the same. It took his group three weeks to start training, which was to be expected. Even though everyone else seemed demoralized, he didn't say a word, as this would be a source of shared comradery within the group. Eventually, their group was finally assembled, and the busses arrived. As the Drill Instructors barked orders, David remained calm, effortlessly carrying his equipment and getting on line while most of his platoon stressed out. He was not picked as the platoon guide, because he had never attended a Junior ROTC program in high school, which was fine by him.

One thing he wasn't prepared for was the noticeable change in expectation he had for how trainees reacted to the Drill Instructors versus how he treated them. He never had any issues during his training before, but there seemed to be an expectation of uncertainty and fear expected from the trainees, something David clearly didn't have. Several Drill instructors challenged him, thinking he wasn't taking training seriously, but after several weeks, he had proven his expertise and understanding beyond their own, something that earned him an unspoken pass by the cadre.

His first physical fitness test was one of those moments, scheduled two weeks upon their arrival. David never failed a fitness test before, but his performance the first time was acceptable, at best. This time, he didn't even get one minute into his two-minute time limit before reaching the maximum score on the pushup and sit-up event. During the two mile run, he didn't stop running until the second fastest runner finished his test at thirteen minutes and six seconds. At this point, David was one lap away from reaching three miles. His peers thought he was just behind the lead, until his time was called out, "David Renado! nine minutes and forty-five seconds! Why the hell did you keep running!" David ignored this question and simply walked while waiting for the rest to finish. Of course, he knew what this meant, he was going to be the point man of A-group during the ability group runs.

During his time at Basic Training, David earned the reputation for being competent, but also a problem child, as he often challenged the cadre when they made mistakes, something no one would really know to catch. However, these mistakes were obvious to him. One privilege he was able to gain was the use of the First Sergeant's weight room in the gym below the bay, something few recruits were given.

Basic rifle marksmanship was the next event he looked forward to, as he hadn't had a chance to handle a weapon in more than five years. In his previous life, he owned many firearms, which included several pistols, revolvers, rifles and shotguns, alongside his more extensive training in other weapons systems. Unfortunately, his training would only involve the M16A2. With decades of experience to pull from, his rifle qualification was a walk in the park, however, he didn't get a perfect score, after all, that would be far too fantastic, even for this story.

In the winter of that year, his time at Basic Training had come to an end, and their graduation was held inside on account of the weather, something David didn't mind. However, he didn't like the idea of taking the bus back to his hometown for holiday leave, as he would much rather get a plane ticket. Unfortunately, he had taken the bus before, and this decision was why he was delayed due to weather, which subsequently resulted in his advanced training assignment with the rest of the late comers.

After two days on the road, David arrived at the bus station, where his mother waited for him in her car. As he carried his bags to the car, his mother rushed out to greet him. "How was training?" she asked, excitedly. "It was about as I expected, but I've got more training after the holidays," he responded. They arrived at the house early in the morning and David immediately went to sleep. The last time David was here, he met up with a few people, to include Sarah, his former coworker, but because he had never pursued her this time around, he had no intention of doing so this time.

After waking up in the early afternoon, he got dressed and immediately drove his car to Summer's house. David knew she would be on holiday leave as well, because even though she started her training three months before he did, her individual training was sixteen weeks long and she would only be fourteen weeks in at this point. David knocked on the door and her father answered. David had never actually seen him up close but recognized him instantly. "Good afternoon, I'm a friend of..." "I know who you are," he interrupted. David gasped. "I saw you in her prom photo, plus she never shuts up about you." David chuckled as her father turned back into the house. Several moments later, Summer came running, nearly tripping over the furniture on the way to the door. He braced himself as she jumped at him, catching her mid-air.

Summer didn't hide her affection, she clung to him as he held her for nearly a minute, waiting for her to say something. "How was training?" he asked. "It's really hard, but at least I'm almost finished," she said in a muffled tone. "Yes, but now you've got college to look forward to." She lowered her head back onto his shoulder, "Don't remind me." Summer invited David into her house and they both went to her room.

Her room was slightly smaller than his but looked more like a bedroom than his did. "How long is your training?" she asked. David smiled before responding, "Eight weeks." "What! Only eight weeks?" she said, shocked at his answer. "Yes, but our jobs are different.

Plus, I'll be going to Airborne school after training, so there is that." Summer sat quietly for a moment, touching his hand. "Where are you going to go when you're done with training?" David spent the next few minutes explaining his next steps, where he'll be going, the dates he'll arrive, even the exact unit of assignment.

Summer smiled, "So, you managed to stay on track, that's good." David rubbed the back of his neck, "Yeah, but in order to make sure, I had to take a bus from the east coast, and I have to take a bus back. At least your training is only an hour away from here." Summer hung her head, a sad look on her face. "What's wrong?" he asked. She sighed before answering, "I don't like being separated from you. I mean, I'll be done with training in a couple of weeks, but then there's college. How long do you think that'll take?" David thought for a moment, "You do have several options, but there are consequences to each one." Summer leaned in, kissing him as he explained, "You could always transfer your college residency to a military hospital, after you get done with the first part." "Can't I just go with you?" she asked. He shook his head, "You can, but you'd have to transfer your reserve unit and put college off for a while. And you can't transfer to active duty, because then we would be on competing career paths, which could backfire." Summer nodded her head, "I see."

David grabbed her by the chin and kissed her, "Finish your training, finish your residency, then come and find me. You already know where I'll be and when."

Summer looked up at him, her eyes wide as he explained her options. "I want you in me so bad right now," she said with a serious tone. David was taken aback. "What? Just because of what I said?" She nodded her head, "You've already gotten everything figured out, and I can't tell you how reassuring it is to not have to wonder about my future, especially with you." David smiled as he rubbed her head. "Let's not get ahead of ourselves, even now, nothing is certain." She nodded.

David had places to go, so he made plans with Summer and left. Approximately twenty minutes later, he pulled up to a familiar white house with green trim. As he approached the door, he could hear loud talking through the window, Krystal was visiting, but at least they weren't arguing. He knocked on the door and Krystal answered. "Good afternoon Krystal, may I come in?" She didn't answer, but instead, turned back to summon her mother. As Laura approached the door, she smiled, "Come in David, good to see you!" Krystal was confused, after all, in this life, she had never actually been formally introduced to David, but as soon as Jennifer saw him, she broke down in tears.

Not showing any concern for her sister or mother, she lunged at him, "David! Oh my god, you're here!" Hugging him tightly. David was worried she was going to start peeing on the spot, so he tried to put her down. "I've been such a good girl, you'd be so proud of me!" she finally sat down. "I've just come to say that I'm home for the holidays and this will actually be the last time I'm here for a while," he announced. The room fell silent, and the women looked at each other as he sat on the couch. "So, are you coming to say goodbye?" Laura asked. "I don't know, I'm just sharing the news," he responded. Jennifer was on the verge of tears, something her mother noticed immediately. "I'm sure he'll come back and visit, plus you still have to finish school," her mother said, trying to calm her down.

The three sat and talked for a few hours before David stood up. "I need to be going, but I'll be sure and visit again before I go." As he walked to his car, Jennifer followed him out, bundled up in a heavy coat and wearing house shoes. "I want to stay with you," she mumbled. David lifted her head and kissed her nose, "Be a good girl and when you're ready, I'll come collect you." She reached up, grabbing his neck as she kissed him desperately. She let go and he got in his car, "I'll make time for you after Christmas," he said before leaving. Jennifer smiled as he drove away, then turned and skipped back to her house.

There was very little he could do with everyone's plans for the holidays, so his opportunities were limited. Ultimately, he decided to invite Summer and Jennifer to a New Years eve party, as this would be the last chance to see either one of them for a while. Summer didn't need to convince her father, but Jennifer had to leverage her good grades and conduct in order to convince her mother, until she finally acquiesced. Truthfully, David was not planning a party, but rather, a small gathering. With the help of one of his former work colleagues, he managed to reserve a space in a historical building downtown, that had been converted into an apartment with a few reservable rooms for short term use. He picked this building, because it was the tallest building in this city.

On the last day of December, David left early to prepare for the night, waiting until early afternoon to pick everyone up. Because Jennifer's house was closest to him, he picked her up first, this time, she packed a change of clothes. After throwing her bag in the trunk, she jumped in the passenger seat and fastened her seatbelt. Truthfully, she had no idea what to expect but wasn't going to be unprepared again. As they left her house, she asked, "Are your parent's home today?" David furled his eyebrow before responding, "Yes, my father is home at the moment, why do you ask?" She looked toward the road, "Because you haven't fucked me in forever and I feel like I'm going to wither and die if you don't." David smiled as he responded, "That's being a bit dramatic, don't you think?" She didn't answer but looked at him with a sad look on her face. "Fine, fine, I'll stop for a bit on the way there, just keep your panties on in the meantime."

David pulled into the driveway of an empty house, two blocks away from his own. David knew this house was abandoned and even knew it would be set for demolition next spring. Luckily, the property was still untouched and completely overgrown with large Ficus trees. However,

Jennifer wouldn't have cared, as soon as he parked, she pulled her panties down from under her skirt and crawled into his lap, as if compelled by some great purpose. Without regard to any form of consideration or decorum, he lowered his seat back as she used her hand to guide him between her legs.

Nearly fifteen minutes later, they finally arrived in front of Summer's house, only three blocks away. David walked to her door as Jennifer sat in the back seat, resting from their recent tryst. As soon as the door opened, Summer rushed him, shouldering her overnight bag. After hugging him, she stopped, looking at him with a puzzled look. "What is it?" he asked. Summer shook her head, "Never mind, I thought I, uh, umm, nothing, forget it." The two walked to the car and as Summer opened the door, her attention immediately went to the back seat, noticing Jennifer. "I thought I smelled something familiar!" David smiled as he started the car, not saying a word. Looking at the two, Summer asked, "You two couldn't wait? Have you no restraint?"

After driving for twenty minutes, he parked next to a tall tan building. The girls looked up as they approached. "Do you know someone who lives here?" Summer asked. "Not exactly, but I do know someone that was able to negotiate with one of the owners." The three rode the elevator to the tenth floor, where it opened up to a short hallway with two doors, one on each side. David unlocked the left door and went inside. Upon entering, the girls began exploring the small apartment. This was in fact a penthouse apartment, but it was very small with only one bedroom and the dining room table shared the same space as the living room. However, the ambiance was quite comforting, and both girls immediately felt at home.

David opened both sets of windows on opposite sides of the apartment before returning to the living room with two small bags, one silver and one blue. Jennifer and Summer blushed as they both knew which bag was theirs without asking. The first item pulled from the bag was a chemise, eliciting a blushing smile from both girls. As Summer was admiring the feel of the chemise against her skin, Jennifer shouted in excitement as she pulled a collar from her bag, startling Summer.

Looking into her own bag, she didn't find a collar, but a Sterling chain choker with a small tag with five symbols engraved. Three circles, one with a line diagonally through the middle, the middle with three dots over top, and the third with a single line top to bottom, and on each end, the Greek Delta. Summer automatically knew what this was and jumped to kiss David, clutching her chain in her hand. David gestured to the bedroom and told them to get dressed as he prepared dinner in the small kitchen. Several minutes later, both girls emerged wearing their chemises, eliciting a smile from David.

After they ate, all three sat in the living room, illuminated only by a small lamp in the corner of the room. Of course, Jennifer was the first to take the initiative, unfastening David's pants as she laid her head on his lap. Summer was on his opposite side, leaning against his shoulder as they spoke hypothetically about their uncertain future, when she noticed Jennifer trying to get David's dick out of his pants. "Are you some kind of nymphomaniac?" she asked. Jennifer looked nervously at Summer before responding, "No, why would you think that?" Summer shook her head. She was aware that their very survival may be dependent on whether David continued to find their company valuable, but Jennifer wasn't desperate, in fact, she seemed completely conquered by him.

With a smile on her face, Summer leaned down to Jennifer's ear and whispered. David watched as Jennifer smiled, sitting up, allowing Summer to straddle David's lap. She wasn't nearly as aggressive as her counterpart, but her desire could be felt no less. Immediately taking him in, she sat firmly on his lap, arms wrapped tightly around him as she occasionally arched her back, pushing her hips down into him. Meanwhile, Jennifer sat to the side, watching Summer grind her body into David as she indulged herself openly.

As Summer reached her climax, her body began to shake as her back arched almost unnaturally, spraying David as she fell backward off of him rather comically. Jennifer chuckled as she crawled toward him to finish him off with her mouth. As he finished, Jennifer wiped the corners of her mouth with her fingers as Summer continued to lie on the floor just below, one leg still on the couch with her chemise bunched up above her abdomen.

After going to bed quite early, the two girls took turns getting their fill of David, who never seemed to tire, even after several hours. As poppers and fireworks went off outside; the three of them, half covered and partially glued together from their recent activities, didn't move much. Jennifer, with her head down by his stomach, gripped his waist, with her legs wrapped around his. Summer, however, wasn't so submissive, her hand resting on his chest as she kept her face much closer to his.

Over the next few days, the weather had gotten much colder, and David would eventually have to leave, this time for his advanced training. The next nine weeks went almost as he remembered with one exception. His platoon was a motley crew of misfits and while each group overlapped, some factions would always fight. The more conservative groups were those divided by basic training assignment. Half of the platoon were in the same basic training company before the winter break, these soldiers often ate together and seldom had conflict. The other group was divided by race, often segregating themselves from others and would even get into fights with the Marines. This group frequently brought hardship for the rest of the platoon and even for David himself. However, this time, he didn't fear their retaliation and even confronted them directly, time and again.

In the following spring, after graduating from his advanced training and Airborne school, his first order of business was to get his car. Something he had to wait for, until after arriving at his first duty assignment.

Appendix: 1

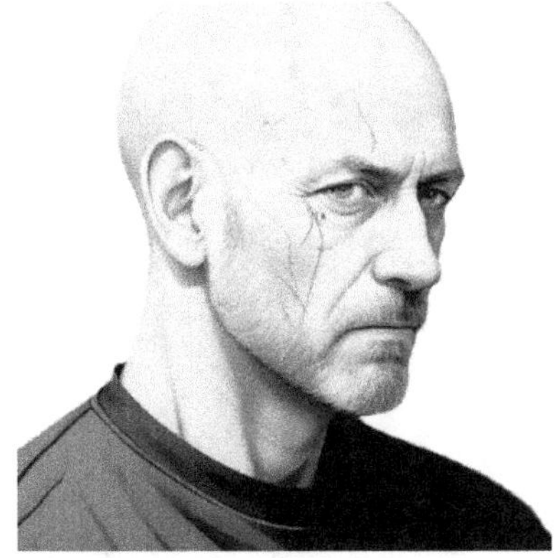

David Renado (53)

Woman on Bus

David Renado (13)

Tiffany Altman

Mother

Father

Jennifer Clarke

Summer Bellarose

Coded Alphabet

Donna

www.ingramcontent.com/pod-product-compliance
Lightning Source LLC
Chambersburg PA
CBHW060624310726
48982CB00003B/666